THE ROARING '20S

A DECADE OF STORIES

EDITED BY JK LARKIN

RED
PENGUIN
Books

The Roaring '20s

Copyright © 2021 by JK Larkin

All rights reserved

Published by Red Penguin Books

Bellerose Village, New York

Library of Congress Control Number: 2021903832

ISBN

Print 978-1-63777-026-9

Digital 978-1-63777-027-6

CONTENTS

1. FLAPPER AND THE CAPTAIN   1
David Lange

2. AN ACT OF SENSELESSNESS   35
Shevaun Cavanaugh Kastl

3. ALIVE IN THE BASEMENT   43
Eric Wayne

4. PERFECT PAIR   55
Amanda Montoni

5. GROWING UP IN THE SUMMER OF '71   73
Debbie De Louise

6. HOLLOW GLITZ   93
Olivia Arieti

7. ANOTHER MOUTH   99
Terri Paul

8. GIRLS JUST WANT TO HAVE FUN   113
Elaine Donadio

9. THE SOCIAL EXPERIMENT   125
Anita Haas

10. POCKET WATCH   133
Robert A. Morris

11. TIME IS HERE AND GONE   139
William John Rostron

About the Editor   159
Also from The Red Penguin Collection   161

1

FLAPPER AND THE CAPTAIN

DAVID LANGE

I slowly made my way along 42nd street, heading toward Grand Central Station, intent on purchasing a one-way ticket back to a town I knew would not understand me. Staying in New York was a bad idea. In a city so large, I thought I might blend in; disappear. And I did, for brief moments here and there. Like thousands of other veterans returning from The Great War, I disembarked the ocean liner that carried us back from Europe, and I was hypnotized by the bright lights and excitement of New York City. The economy was booming and I knew I would eventually find my niche. With cane in hand, I hobbled the streets in search of a place where I belonged. Sure, I'd find a joint, here and there, that was willing to toss a few coins at me, but it was always barely enough dough to pay my rent. Just when I thought I had picked a winner, my horse would come up lame and I'd be out on the street again. I tried to sign on with the post office, delivering airmail. I had flown during the war and, even with my bum leg, I thought I could still fly. I got as far as an interview once, and then a door slammed in the next room and I fell to the floor, screaming, curled up in a fetal position. The docs called it "shell shock" and no employer wanted to have anything to do with me. My body was only partially broken—I'd been splinted back together after two serious crashes. They told me I was lucky to be alive. I wasn't so sure. The gunfire; the shelling; the explosions and the smoke; the smell of death in the air—it takes its toll, don't it? I had hocked nearly all of my possessions, hoping to reunite with them when my fortune took a turn for the better. I knew better days were just beyond the horizon. I've been telling myself that for five years now. I'd seen those sheiks driving Broadway in their ritzy automobiles and those gorgeous dames, bedecked in jewels and furs, and I wanted a taste of that life. I felt the world owed it to me. The world threw a wet blanket over that dream in a hurry. The only thing I had left was my Army Air Service flying jacket and, if the winter wind wasn't biting, I'd have probably hocked that, as well. 1923 had been an exciting year for many New Yorkers. The New York Yankees and the New York Giants played each other in the World Series and that fella Ruth really made a showing with a .368 batting average and three home runs to his name. He helped lead the Bronx Bombers to their first World Series win. I shared in the excitement but the joy was only temporary and I knew it wasn't going to sustain me through a cold and rainy winter.

As if on cue, the rain started falling moments after I had checked out of the hotel. It was a dark and cold night. Rain began to soak through the canvas of my pack, threatening the only change of clothes I had available. I quickened my pace, but my cane slipped as I stepped off the wet curb and I stumbled and fell into a puddle in the street. I felt utterly defeated as I lay there, curled up; honking horns and angry shouts roaring like thunder in my ears. I was frozen. My tears were diluted by the rainwater streaming down my face. And that's when I felt the warmth of her hand.

"Pool's closed, Fly Boy. Here, take my hand and climb on out." It was an angel's voice. Had I been hit by a car? Was I dead? The cold pavement and rain felt real enough. No dice... this flier was still grounded. I regained my feet, never letting go of the stranger's hand yet fearing to look her, or anyone, in the eyes. I was still trembling and I learned, years ago, to hide my darkness. With her free hand, my rescuer slowly turned my chin until my head was facing hers. I looked down, still reluctant to make eye contact. "Once you're done checking out the goods, how about you send those baby blues back up here?" I immediately felt embarrassed. I was blushing as I lifted my head to look her in the eyes. What a dish! She was stunning! Her short, black, bobbed hair formed a sharp contrast with her fair complexion and ruby red lips. And those eyes! So blue and filled with a mischievous excitement! I was transfixed. She gently squeezed my hand and led me, willingly, along the wet sidewalk toward a nearby hotel. "What do you say we move out of the rain?" I still wasn't speaking so I just nodded and accompanied her beneath the fringed canopy at the entrance of an extravagant hotel.

Collecting myself, I finally spoke. "Hey, I suppose I should thank you for rescuing me from drowning. I'm Jimmy, by the way. What's your name?" The woman briefly considered my question and then, with flirtatious eyes, responded.

"What would you like it to be?" I was taken aback.

"Well, you kind of look like a Trixie."

"Gosh, you're a regular Harry Houdini, aren't you! You guessed my name on the very first try." I was skeptical.

"Sure. That's what they all call me... Houdini."

"I like Jimmy better. Okay if I just go with that?" I took her hand and kissed it gently.

"Jimmy it is." Trixie seemed a little surprised by the kiss. She curtsied and smiled.

"Well now, 'Jimmy-it-is,' the night is young and I couldn't bear to face it alone. How about we get you into some dry clothes and you escort me through my evening of drunken debauchery."

"That's all well and fine, but aren't you forgetting about one little thing?"

"What's that, dearest?"

"A little thing called the 18th Amendment... Prohibition." A devious grin slowly formed upon Trixie's lovely face.

"Let's get you dry."

"Where do you intend to do that?" I asked. Trixie's eyes drifted upward to the hotel towering above us.

"This is my hotel. We'll just get you a room for the night and I'll have the concierge dry out all your clothes and find you something suitable for the evening." I was surprised, and a little confused, but I wasn't about to turn down this charitable offer from one of the most beautiful creatures I've ever seen. I nodded my approval.

We walked into the hotel lobby and the staff immediately treated Trixie like royalty. Hardly a moment passed before we had a room and assurance that fresh clothes would be delivered within the next thirty minutes. We entered the elevator where the smartly dressed operator tipped his hat and greeted Trixie. "Good evening, Miss Beauchamp. Seventh floor?"

"Lucky seven, Reggie." Trixie winked at the operator who coyly looked away.

"You might want to be careful where you flash that smile, Miss; you're likely to be breaking hearts from here to Los Angeles."

"You're sweet, Reggie. Thank you, dear." Trixie pulled some money from her purse and stuffed a few bills in Reggie's vest pocket. "That's for the heart doctor. You can keep the change."

Trixie's room was just across the hall from mine. I asked if she wouldn't mind if I took a warm bath before our night out. I was still chilled to the bone from my aqueous winter mishap. Trixie told me that she'd expect no less. She instructed me to leave the wet clothes outside my door, to include any wet clothes in my bag. The hotel provided robes that would serve me while I awaited the turnaround. I must admit, it had been a very long time since I had such a wonderful bath, and never in such luxurious accommodations. The hotel was warm and welcoming and my room was spectacular. I was surveying the art upon the wall when a knock came at the door. It was Trixie, bearing a pressed tuxedo upon an oak hanger. I suggested she pass my garment through the partially opened door since I was only wearing a robe, but she was undeterred. Trixie practically pushed her way in. I wasn't used to the brashness but I wasn't about to turn her out. Her long fur coat was unbuttoned, revealing a tightly fitting short black dress–the hemline just above the knees. Several strings of pearls adorned her neckline. A jewel-encrusted headband with a colorful feather protruding completed the look. My jaw dropped. Without me ever saying a word, Trixie smiled and told me she was flattered. My expression spoke the words I could not.

Retreating from view, I changed into the tuxedo. Trixie seemed amused by my modesty. I had to wonder what kind of fellas she usually associated with. I suppose it didn't matter.

"You look like a million dollars, Fly Boy. The fit's not bad. I had to guess at your sizes but, well... I'm pretty good at sizing up a man." Again, her expression was slightly suggestive. "The night isn't getting any younger; let's hit the town." And that's exactly what we did. The rain was subsiding as the hotel doorman hailed us a cab. I was a willing passenger on this voyage to the unknown —an excursion of growing peculiarity being led by a beautiful and mysterious stranger whom I had only just met. My curiosity was peaking as Trixie led me to a small barbershop in a less-traveled corner of the city. She held my hand, giggling as she led me around the corner to a side door in the adjacent alley. I might have thought this to be some clever mugging scheme but I didn't believe that even Trixie was mad enough to dress me up in a Tuxedo so that she could make off with the twelve dollars in my tattered wallet. She had me step back and muttered a few words at the formidable iron door. The door slowly opened and Trixie motioned me to join her. We descended a dingy cement stairway, dimly lit by a single bulb. As we approached another sturdy door, at the bottom, I could faintly hear the unmistakable sounds of jazz music. Once through the final portal, I was awestruck by not only the size of the room but also the intensity of human energy within the large subterranean cavern.

So, this was one of those "speakeasies" I had read about. I had never been to one. They were illegal. They were, as I understand, also very common. I have to believe the police turned a blind eye to most of the establishments; more so if the owner had the right connections in Tammany Hall or slipped a little dough to the underpaid cops walking the local beat. The atmosphere was vibrant and the booze ran freely. I offered to buy Trixie a drink, fearing that she'd be beating me to the punch if I didn't, but before either of us could drop any coin, the owner appeared and gave Trixie a big hug, yelling over to the bartender that our drinks for the night were to be on the house. Who was this girl?!

We grabbed a corner table and sat down with our drinks. Trixie asked a lot about my flying experience and I dutifully answered, leaving out all of the darker memories that still haunted me from the war. Before I realized it, I had nearly provided my complete biography and had yet to learn a single significant fact about the woman I was sharing the evening with. I was about to turn the tables when I noticed Trixie's feet tapping uncontrollably beneath the table.

"C'mon, Jimmy, let's dance," she beckoned with youthful

excitement. Oh, how I wanted to. But, after having recently failed to negotiate a curb with my bum leg, I thought it best I turn down the offer. Trixie was disappointed and she let me know it with her best pouty face. "Oh, lover. Mind if I do? You may need to beat the wolves away with that cane of yours." I laughed and shooed her off to the dance floor just as a waiter was bringing us a second round of drinks. Boy, did that taste good. It'd been too long.

Trixie lit up the room. Fox Trot, Shimmy, the Charleston; she seamlessly transitioned between dances and all her admirers stepped back to watch the show. I watched, in awe. And then I slowly got to my feet. Trixie saw me and skipped over to the band leader, whispering something in his ear. She returned to the center of the room, reached her hand out across the emptiness toward where I was standing, and called my name. "Jimmy?" I stood there, contemplating. A slow, repeating chant grew in volume throughout the establishment.

"Jimmy, Jimmy, Jimmy..." Trixie just stood there; her arm outstretched; her eyes enticing me ever closer. With my cane steadying me, I walked toward the center of the floor where I joined Trixie. The speakeasy erupted in applause and cheers. Trixie carefully took my cane and gently set it on the floor as the band began to play a slow tune. Trixie held me tight and I returned the affection, occasionally having to steady myself in hold. She didn't mind. As we slowly swayed across the floor, Trixie was more than happy to be my emotional and physical support. After the music ended, we just stood there, holding each other tightly, our eyes locked in meaningful union. Across the room, a table tipped over, shattering several glass bottles and the blissful serenity of the moment. I fell to the floor, my heart racing, sweat pouring down my face. The proprietor yelled over at the offenders and then ran over to attend to me. Trixie waved him off.

"I've got it from here, Louie. Thank you, darling."

"Sure thing, Trixie. I'm really sorry about that."

"Don't be sorry. I had a lovely evening." Trixie knelt down beside me and grasped my hand. She looked back at Louie. "We had a lovely evening." The band resumed their vibrant jazz tunes as Trixie and I made our way up the stairs and back to the street.

"I'm so sorry, Trixie. I didn't mean to spoil your evening. If you want to go back without me, that's fine; I understand."

"You didn't spoil a thing. I loved the way you held me as we danced. Besides, I'm not done with you yet."

"You're not?"

"No. If you're willing to stick around another day, I think I can promise you an experience you'll never forget." Well, that sure sounded enticing. I wonder what Trixie saw in me? How did a glamorous dame like her get stuck with a broken man like me? She could have gone home with anyone in that club. New York was her oyster.

We hailed another cab and returned to the hotel. Trixie refused to release any more details of her master plan until we were alone together in the hotel. Up on the seventh floor, Trixie accompanied me to my room. Once there, she reached into her purse and pulled out two impressive monographed envelopes. Each was sealed with red wax; a heraldic figure embossed upon the seal.

"What in the world are those?" I asked.

"My ulterior motive. I hope you're not offended." I looked at Trixie, confused, but definitely not offended. "You see, I have two invitations for a grand gala at the Meyer Mansion on Long Island and I am sorely in need of an escort."

"And you chose me?"

"I needed a dashing co-conspirator and, unfortunately, Rudolph Valentino was otherwise engaged this weekend. Besides, in your smashing new tuxedo, I'm not sure even Rudy could measure up. Please tell me you'll come." I paused, for dramatic effect, but my mind was made up even before Trixie's formal invitation was complete.

"Sure thing. It would be an honor. But no falling tables, okay?"

"I can't swear to the steadfastness of the furniture but I can promise you I'll be there to lend a hand."

"Deal." I smiled and extended my hand.

"Deal." Trixie ignored my hand and pulled me in for a long hug and a kiss on the cheek. We chatted for a while longer before Trixie kissed me goodnight. I watched as she danced across the hall to her room, stopping only briefly to wave and blow me a final kiss before exiting the scene. What a gal!

I did not sleep well. My nights were still haunted by the irrepressible images of my wartime experiences. All the same, I was awake and ready for the bugle-sounding Reveille—a wakening call I'd not heard in a great many years. Old habits die hard. I was fairly confident that I wouldn't see Trixie until later in the day. We had prearranged to meet in the lobby at half-past five. At six, I returned to the seventh floor and knocked on Trixie's door. An elderly man opened the door, awoken from his afternoon nap. I gracefully absorbed his retribution, apologized, and beat a hasty retreat toward the lobby. I pulled out my pocket watch and considered whether or not I had been stood up by the prettiest girl in New York City. I wouldn't have blamed her. Was it the alcohol speaking when she offered the invitation? I made up my mind to maintain my position until forcibly removed. Fortunately, it never came to that. At a quarter to seven, Trixie returned, looking absolutely ravishing in a shimmering white gown that hugged the curves of her body as it draped its way down toward her ankles. Lovely silver snowflakes were embroidered across the gown and I'm quite convinced that Venus, herself, might have been jealous were she to behold the vision before me. I half expected an apology for her late arrival but I should have known better. I had lived by the clock for too many years—it drove my actions; the ticking gears pounding in my head and reminding me of time lost and dwindling possibilities for the future. Trixie was no slave to time. Time bent to her will and bowed before her as she confidently strode by.

"Be a dear and retrieve my coat, would you? And no flirting with the coat check girl." Trixie handed me a receipt and I forgot all about the time.

"But of course, good lady." I bowed, regally. Trixie got a kick out of that.

"See, I knew Valentino had nothing on you."

With coats in hand, we set off on our adventure. Trixie had arranged for a private car to take us across the Queensboro Bridge to the ritzy Gold Coast of Long Island. She wasn't about to show up, dressed to the nines, in a taxi cab. Trixie was all class.

The Meyer Mansion, presently ruled over by investment banker Franz Meyer, sat upon a sprawling 400-acre estate, bejeweled by fountains and gardens. Meyer was well known for his lavish parties and celebrated each season with an appropriately themed event. The silver snowflakes on Trixie's gown and the white feathers adorning her sparkling tiara now made sense—I was escorting the Snow Queen to the Winter Ball. Of course.

As we pulled into the large, circular, driveway, an attendant leapt forth and opened the door on Trixie's side of the vehicle while another attended to my door. Out of the corner of my eye, I saw Trixie whisper something to our driver and slip him what looked to be a hundred dollar note—more dough than most honest working men earned in a week. I still wondered where Trixie came by her money. I thought it better not to ask.

Ascending the spectacular marble stairs leading to the grand entry, I could already see that the booze was flowing freely. I would not have been at all surprised if the spectacular fountains on the premises were spewing liquor. With that kind of dough, I'm sure all the police departments within a hundred-mile radius were incentivized to overlook indulgences on the Meyer Estate. Half undressed women were chased by amorous suitors as the band set the musical tone for frivolity. Ice sculptures adorned the interior of the home, watching over impossibly fantastic buffet tables set beneath luminous crystal chandeliers. Marble and gold; silk and fine lace. Every corner of the mansion screamed excess. I felt terribly uncomfortable. This was Trixie's world, not mine. What was I thinking? I grew more taciturn while Trixie swept us through the corridors, winking and waving. The laughing and shouting; drums beating and trumpets blaring; a thousand unnamed faces shouting inaudible greetings—it was too much. I could feel the sweat soaking my shirt. My hands were starting to tremble. I wasn't sure I was going to be able to keep it together, yet I had to try—for Trixie.

"Trixie, I'm not sure I can do this." I felt awful but I didn't want to embarrass Miss Beauchamp in front of her social friends. For all I knew, they were the source of her inexhaustible financial reserves. With each passing moment, the crowd seemed to grow denser and the noise more intense. Trixie pulled me through a hallway that led to a fantastic balcony overlooking the Long Island Sound. We stood there for a while, admiring the stars and ignoring the occasional gleeful screams coming from the nearby garden as frolickers set about destroying Eden. "Trixie, I . . ." I hadn't finished my apology before I felt the warmth of Trixie's hand tenderly squeezing mine.

"Shhh. I know." Her voice was gentle and soothing. "It's alright . . . truly." We stood together in silence. Eventually, she released my hand and we turned toward each other. "I need you to fight for me, just a little bit longer. Please fight." I was confused. What did she mean by "fight?" "Jimmy, do you think you can find your way through this rat maze and to the field beyond the statuary garden?"

"I suppose so." I would have found my way through the Minotaur's Labyrinth if Trixie had requested it.

"I need you to do this for me, Jimmy. Go to the field and find the car that we came in. It'll be parked near the statue of Icarus. The doors will be unlocked. In fifty minutes, I need you to start the engine and keep it running."

"Is that fifty minutes of Trixie time?" I quipped. Trixie gave me a friendly shove which, I'm embarrassed to say, nearly knocked me over.

"No, lover. That's fifty minutes of Captain Douglas time." It was the first time Trixie had actually used my former rank. Outside an off-hand remark I made the day before, it never came up in conversation. Trixie hadn't forgotten. I stood a little taller.

"Five zero minutes. You got it. Should I even bother inquiring?"

"No." Trixie paused for a moment to consider. "Cold night, and all—a little extra engine warming never hurts, right?"

"Sure. It'll be warm." I welcomed the assignment, even as my mind grappled for an explanation.

We parted and I fought my way upstream against the floodwaters of humanity pouring toward the back end of the mansion. Trixie disappeared below the waves. I could feel my heart pounding and the symptoms of another attack coming on. I was suffocating within the unchecked sprawl of humanity. Like a Doughboy on the front lines, I was fighting for every inch of progress. I was fighting to keep my head together. I can't crack. I can't give up. I've got to pull through for Trixie. It was a close-run thing, but I finally made my way out of the Meyer Mansion and beyond the grasping arms of a half dozen fried flappers who seemed ready to engage in amorous escapades with any gentleman who would have them. Making whoopee was not on my agenda for the evening. Clear of humanity, I searched in the lamplit darkness of the night for Icarus. Icarus, the chump whose wings melted when he flew too close to the sun—he fell from the sky, drowning in the sea below. I could empathize.

I found our vehicle, a 1923 Maxwell Model 25. I was surprised it was still here. Trixie must have paid the driver to stick around. Perhaps he was one of the fellas chasing dames through the garden? Thirty minutes remaining. I searched the vehicle for keys. There'd be no warm-up without the keys. On the passenger side, I was surprised to find my leather flying jacket. What was that doing here? Even more surprising, the keys to the Maxwell were in the pocket of my jacket. I strained in the dim light to read the hands of my pocket watch. With key in hand, I waited. I could see a stream of headlights flowing along the drive leading to the property. This party was far from over and was unlikely to reach its crescendo until the wee hours of the morning. I was honestly surprised that Trixie wasn't planning on dancing through to dawn. Ten minutes remaining. Five. Four. Three. I could swear I heard some gunshots coming from the mansion. That was probably fireworks. Two. One. With no one to evaluate my precision, I still took great pride in firing up the Maxwell at fifty minutes, to the second. The car shuddered back to life, like a lion shaking off the night's chill. I admired the night sky, my "challenging" assignment complete. More shots. Bells ringing. Indiscernible shouts emanating from here and there. I was losing it. I was fighting but I was losing it. My demons would not let go. My hands were trembling and tears were streaming down my cheeks when I saw a shadowy figure running rapidly toward the car. It was Trixie! Heels in her left hand and a leather satchel in her right, she was making record time across the grassy field. She reached the car, gasping for air.

"Can you drive? Jimmy, can you drive?" I fumbled for words.

More shots rang out through the night. Searchlights were panning the grounds and I could hear the distant sound of police sirens. "Slide over, baby. I think I'd better take the wheel. You've had too much to drink." I hadn't touched a drop all night but I scooted over to the passenger side and let Trixie take the wheel. A spray of mud flew from the rear tires as Trixie put the car in gear and floored the accelerator. We were off the property in minutes and heading south on back roads. I was beside myself. I felt a terrible shame for failing. I was completely bewildered by Trixie's actions and the significance of the events of the past hour.

Up ahead, we saw the headlights of several vehicles approaching us at a high speed. With sirens wailing, there was no doubt these were responding coppers. Much to my dismay, Trixie pulled off the road, sliding in behind some trees, and turned off the headlights on our vehicle. The police cars had no sooner passed than Trixie was back on the road and doing some high-speed driving of her own. A fog was beginning to settle upon the island, but Trixie raced onward, undeterred. I felt uneasy about the situation.

"Trixie, what have you gotten us into? What did you do?" Trixie was silent. I thought she may not have heard my question above the roar of the engine or perhaps because she was focused on negotiating every bend in the road without sacrificing speed. Despite my concerns, my anxiety seemed to be fading—the movement and the roar of the engine had a strangely calming effect on me. I looked out ahead. The stars had long-since disappeared; the fog was thickening. Several minutes later, Trixie finally responded.

"Do you trust me, Jimmy? Please tell me you trust me."

"Well, sure I trust you, Trixie." My response was more a reflex than a considered position. The truth was, I wasn't sure who to trust anymore and I had little reason to trust the mysterious beauty who appeared out of the dark just the night before; told me nearly nothing substantial about her own affairs; whisked me away upon a surreal journey into the lifestyle of the rich and powerful; and now appeared to be fleeing from the police.

"You do? You trust me, Jimmy? You really trust me?" I knew I wasn't going to pull the wool over this dame's eyes. She was too smart for that. Trixie could read me like a book.

"I don't have to trust you. I love you. I love you and I believe in you."

"You're a fool for falling in love me with, Jimmy." Trixie reached over with her right arm and gently squeezed my shoulder, never taking her eyes off the road.

"Then let me die a fool." The conversation stopped. I'd follow Trixie to the sun even though it meant my wings of wax would melt and I'd fall to my death. I would die for this woman, a thousand times over.

Roosevelt Field?! What were we doing at Roosevelt Field? Trixie slowed the vehicle and slowly drove over to one of the hangers on the quiet airfield. At this time of night, the airfield was nearly lifeless. She turned off the engine and sat there in silence.

"Well now, I guess this is the moment of truth." Trixie was searching for words; she seemed uncharacteristically ill-prepared for the moment. "I stole something, Jimmy; something that didn't belong to Franz Meyer and his crooked mob; something that my family swore to protect. I know you think we're running from the coppers but the cops are the least of our worries. By now, there's probably two dozen cars searching the Island for us... cars filled with men who don't ask questions; men who don't value life. If they find us, they'll bump us off; both of us. And they've got connections. They've got the police and the local government in their pocket. They're going to shut down the bridges and set up checkpoints along all the major roads. They'll be monitoring the ferries and tightening the noose around us until we've got

nowhere to run. They'll trap us like rats in a barrel and then..."
Trixie stopped to wipe a tear out of her eye.

"What's in the hanger, Trixie?"

"Come on, let me show you." We walked through a side door
and I couldn't help but smile when I looked upon a beautifully
maintained war surplus Curtiss JN-4 biplane; a "Jenny." I had
flown Jennys during my training here in the States before I got
shipped overseas to fly fighters with the Air Service in the war. I
knew how to fly her, but that was years ago. I grew anxious as I
understood my purpose. I was the missing puzzle piece. I was
Trixie's ticket off this island prison; I was the guy supposed to
carry her and her prize over the moat around the citadel. Maybe I
should have felt used... or betrayed. But I didn't. Instead, I felt as if
I had been given purpose. This was my last chance to be the
knight in shining armor that I hoped I might be as a naïve second
lieutenant heading off to war. Trixie looked over at me, assessing
my condition, physically and mentally. "Can you fly her, Captain
Douglas?" Captain Douglas. She called me Captain Douglas
again.

"Get the door on that side of the hanger, Trixie; I'll get this
side." We opened the hanger doors. I still had no idea what the
plan was but the clock was ticking in my head and I knew every
second mattered. "Where to, princess?" Trixie pulled out a folded
chart with two spots marked. The destination appeared to be
along the coast in southern Maine. That was a long haul.

"We're not going to make it there on a tank of gas, Trixie."

"No, we won't. This middle mark is a refueling stop. The
landing zone will be marked by three bonfires. The destination
field will also be marked by three bonfires." The chart had towns,
roads, and rail tracks marked but, in the darkness and haze, I
wasn't confident I would have the required visual references to
safely navigate the route. I was going to ask if Trixie would

consider waiting until morning, but the distant sound of multiple car engines removed any doubt that we were in a "now or never" moment. My hand began trembling, but I hid it behind my back.

"Trixie, I'm going to need your help to get this bird breathing."

"Wait, you're not ready yet." Trixie ran to the car and came running back with my leather flying jacket. She slid off my tuxedo jacket. My hand was still trembling and it was getting worse. Trixie didn't say a word as she helped me into my flight jacket. She held both my hands and leaned in to kiss me on the lips. "For Le Capitaine." Her French accent was nearly perfect. I was in seventh heaven. She spoke softly, "I trust you, too, Jimmy." I could have stared into those beautiful eyes all night long, but I knew we had only minutes.

"Thank you." I paused. "Trixie, I'm going to need you to pull down quickly on that side of the propeller when I signal you. After you give it a good pull, I'm going to try to start the engine. Once I do, back away quickly and come around to this side and climb up the wing into the front seat." In the distance, we could see the headlights from at least three vehicles rapidly coming down the road. "On the seat, you'll find a leather cap and some goggles. I suggest you put those on to help keep any leaking oil off your face." I looked out the hanger door and then back toward Trixie. "Well, I suppose there's not much more to say and not near enough time to say it, so let's get to dancing." I hopped in the back seat and, when I was ready for the start, signaled down to Trixie. Like an old pro, she spun the wooden propeller blade counter-clockwise, and smoke spewed from the engine as it came to life. Trixie quickly made it into the front seat with her mysterious satchel and we were on the move. I expeditiously taxied the aircraft toward the runway. The ominous black cars were now heading directly toward us. I could faintly hear the rat-tat-tat of Tommy guns over the familiar music of the Jenny's engine. A bullet whizzed by my head; I could hear it. I remained focused. Reaching the runway, I pushed the throttle forward and accelerated, bullets still racing past. Finally, the wheels left the earth and we were flying. The gunfire faded as we disappeared into the fog and I gently banked right to pick up a northeasterly heading. I thought to calm myself only to realize that my mind was already at ease. I was caught up in the euphoria of the moment—the sheer joy of flying. I gently banked to the left and right; the engine purring beautifully up front; the controls we're responsive and obedient. Occasionally, Trixie would turn to look back at me—her excitement radiating through her glorious smile. I didn't need to ask—this was her first time.

I flew low, straining to pick up the lights of towns along the way or any vehicle headlights that might indicate a major road. A set of railroad tracks proved to be a godsend—I followed them along the coast of Connecticut and into Massachusetts. When no visual cues were available, I relied upon a compass heading and elapsed time to determine my approximate location. The cloud deck seemed to be thinning out as I progressed along my route. Finally, as promised, I saw the glowing flames of three large bonfires in the distance. I breathed a sigh of relief as I began the gentle descent back to earth. I flew toward the flames until I saw a small airstrip in a clearing. I circled once to look for obstructions and then began my approach for landing. We bounced, ever so slightly, upon contact with the ground but I have to admit, I was pretty darn pleased with my first landing in half a decade. I stopped the aircraft at the end of the field, near a small shack. I had no sooner cut the engine than two burley-looking brutes came running out of the shack, waving pistols and yelling for me to get out of the aircraft and keep my hands in the air. Trixie shouted back at them, in French, and the atmosphere quickly changed to a more congenial one. The two men, speaking in

English but with French accents, both apologized and helped Trixie and me out of the aircraft and over toward a small campfire where we shared bread and Brie cheese along with a glass of wine. One of the men set about refueling the Jenny. Our conversation remained cordial but nondescript. Who were they? What was going on here? Had I somehow involved myself in an international spy ring? Was I the good guy or the bad guy? Was I Trixie's fella or just some stooge, duped into being an accomplice in some fantastic heist?

As we sat by the fire, I was offered another glass of wine. The man thanked me for my help and told me that a car would be made available for me in the morning.

"What do you mean, a car will be made available for me?" I waved off the second glass of wine.

"Monsieur, you have done us a great service, tonight. Your job here is done and we all thank you. I'll be taking over from here." Over my dead body! I didn't actually say that. I quickly got up from my position by the fire and nearly fell over. My cane was still sitting in the corner of a hanger on Long Island. My feeble attempt to stand wasn't helping the cause.

"Now listen here," I objected; but Trixie cut me off, mid-sentence, and turned to the man, speaking forcefully in the silkiest French accent I had ever heard. I didn't understand a word. Clearly, Jacques did. He slowly stood, bowed, and apologized for the misunderstanding.

"Forgive me, please, mon capitaine, I was not aware that you would be continuing on from here. A thousand pardons." Jacques saluted me from where he stood.

Trixie looked at me and smiled. "I can only imagine you must be having a hard time with this. Would you mind if I drop the New York accent?"

"You're not from around here, are you? Who are you?"

"Later, my love." She spoke softly now with a beautiful French accent. "I've given you little reason to trust me but I beg of you, please, don't give up on me now." Trixie extended her hand and I accepted it. I wasn't going to let her down... not now. Her expression turned from serious to silly as she asked us not to look as she went behind the shed to relieve herself. We were gentlemen and we gave the woman her privacy. With the Jenny filled with gas and ready for the next leg of the journey, we climbed on board and Jacques gave the propeller a good spin to help get the engine started. Having previously reviewed the navigational chart, I was confident I could use the brilliant light of the moon to follow the coastline to our final destination, provided the clouds cooperated. They did. Sunrise was still several hours away but a glorious moon lit our way, casting a million sparkling gems upon the surface of the waters below. The coastline was easily visible. I followed it north. At one point, I passed abeam a large flock of geese. Both Trixie and I admired the beauty of the scene. Just before dawn, I picked up the glow of fires out ahead. At first, they burned as one before eventually resolving themselves into the familiar pattern of the three marker beacons that would guide us home. Again, I descended and circled the area. There was no airstrip; only a large grassy field amidst a clearing in the trees. Trixie pointed downward; her voice inaudible over the engine. I responded with a thumbs up. The landing was a little bumpier than the last, as the field was not a prepared airstrip, but, as they say, any landing you can walk away from is a good one.

A sea fog was rolling in with the tide and I thanked my lucky stars that it was gracious enough to follow me through the door. Trixie lithely hopped out of the Jenny and ran off toward the wooded area just to the side of the field. I was tired and very stiff; I felt twice my age. Slowly, I climbed out of the cockpit and down off the wing. I had barely made it down before Trixie came running back with a large stick.

"You're cane, mon capitaine." Her smile was lovely and made me forget the pain. I thanked Trixie and steadied myself with the walking stick. I looked around the field. No shack; no Frenchmen sipping wine around a warm fire; just the still of the early morning. The visibility was rapidly degrading. There wasn't going to be a third flight. I shivered and looked over toward Trixie. I wasn't sure what to say.

"Looks like we made it." That was the best I could come up with. Trixie smiled and took my left hand.

"Walk with me." We walked to the edge of the wood and then followed a small dirt path that worked its way through the pines. We ascended a hill and then continued through the trees, descending into a thickening fog. I heard it first—the sea—the soothing music of waves kissing the shore. We were hardly free of the woods before the beautiful Atlantic came into view. Trixie led me, carefully, over to a large rock where we both sat to take our rest. I had a sinking feeling that our time together was nearing an end. I no longer desired to know the answers to the thousand questions racing through my brain; all I wanted was to keep the dream alive.

"This is it? Isn't it?"

"Not quite. I believe I owe you a story." I sat quietly, reveling in the presence of the lovely flapper who had won my heart. I wanted to memorize every feature of her face; the way she spoke; the way she made me feel. I dreaded losing a single detail to the onslaught of time. Trixie looked down and laughed. "You're never going to believe what I tell you. You don't have to."

"Then I'll believe in you." Trixie blushed at my words and held my hand as she spoke.

"Permit me, then, to take you back in time... a great many years

ago. Two French pilgrims returning from the Holy Land took their
rest in the ruins of a small abbey along the pilgrimage route. The
night was cold and wet and what remained of the abbey afforded
them protection from the elements. In the far corner of the abbey,
they heard a man sobbing. The pilgrims went to investigate and
found an inconsolable beggar, hunched over the lifeless body of a
young girl. The beggar explained that the child was his granddaughter and that she had been foraging for food when she was
set upon by a band of thieves who stole the fruits she had
collected and beat her cruelly, leaving her for dead beside the
nearby stream. The old man searched for days before finally
coming upon his granddaughter's body. Death had stolen all but
her last heartbeat. The man carried his beloved granddaughter,
not quite fourteen years of age, back to the ruined abbey that they
had made into a home. The child remained unconscious and
withered slowly, her breath becoming ever-shallower. The
pilgrims begged the old man to let them attend to her. He was
weak and had not eaten in days, himself. He refused to let the
child leave his arms. The pilgrims prayed that night and each was
visited by a fantastic dream whilst they slept. When the dawn
came, the pilgrims thought to share the details of their dreams
with one another. They were stunned to find the dreams were one
and the same. Each dreamed of unearthing a beautiful chalice of
gold, buried beneath a stone lily, and that the powers of that vessel
might return life to the withering body of the beggar's grandchild.
When they shared the details of their extraordinary dream with
the beggar, he sobbed uncontrollably. But these were not the
lamenting tears of a grieving guardian but the joyous tears of one
touched by angels. With a quivering hand, he pointed a bony
finger toward the northeast corner of the abbey and informed the
pilgrims that there was, on that spot, a large stone with a carved
lily upon it. The pilgrims fashioned makeshift digging tools from

the remains of an iron gate and set about excavating around the lily. They dug for the better part of the day until they uncovered a lavishly decorated rosewood box. When they opened the box, they were astonished to see the beautiful golden chalice from their dreams. The cup glowed with an unearthly light. The old beggar pleaded for them to waste no time in filling the cup with water from the nearby stream. The men raced to the stream and complied with the beggar's wish. They returned with the chalice, filled with the cool, clear water, and handed it to the old man. He slowly poured the water across his granddaughter's parched lips and into her mouth. Dipping his finger into the water, he made the sign of a cross upon the young girl's forehead and then he kissed her, lovingly. The girl's eyes slowly opened and she gasped for air. Her body shuddered as Death fled to reap his harvest upon other fields. The pilgrims looked on, in disbelief. The old man cried and thanked the pilgrims for saving his granddaughter's life. In return, he offered the men the chalice. Grateful as they were, these pilgrims were not greedy men. They not only turned down the offer but they left nearly all their food supplies with the old man and his granddaughter. The next morning, they continued on their journey toward home. That night, as they camped just off the road, they were startled to see the beggar's granddaughter running toward them, tears in her eyes. Her clothes were tattered and she bore a leather satchel over her shoulder. She raced over to the pilgrims and embraced them both, telling an awful tale of how the bandits had returned and killed her grandfather. Hearing their approach, the old man placed the golden chalice in the leather satchel and bid her to run as fast as she could to find the pilgrims who had showed them kindness; for only in their care could he be sure the child would be protected. Together, they returned to France. The pilgrims not only held true to their oath to protect the young girl but they carefully hid the chalice in a small abbey not far from the city of Lille. And there it remained, protected through the centuries."

I was spellbound by Trixie's story; more so by the sparkle in her eye as she shared the tale. Her lovely French accent just added to the mystique. "What happened next, Trixie? Did anyone ever find the chalice? What happened to the girl?"

"Ah, so I haven't put you to sleep with my little bedtime story. I'm glad." Trixie continued. "The abbey prospered for years but eventually was abandoned when the order that cared for it disappeared. Some say they left when a plague devastated their order; others claim they were persecuted and forced to flee. There are no remaining records to tell us the true story but legend maintains that some members survive and that these few persist in protecting the secrets of the chalice. Lovely story, no? What we do know is that the German forces occupied that part of France during The Great War. Wherever they went, the Germans collected artwork and treasures from the lands they pillaged. The 'spoils of war.' The old abbey was turned into a fortification of sorts and it was severely damaged during an engagement with French forces. This holy ground is now littered with shell casings and unexploded ordnance—it's far too dangerous to visit. It's very sad. Very sad."

"So, do you think the chalice is still there, buried under all the rubble?"

"Oh no, it's not there. It's safe now."

"How do you know, Trixie?"

"Well, you see, after the war, the Germans sold off much of their captured booty to help pay for their war debts. Rich collectors, of questionable repute, were willing to pay top dollar for the masterpieces and treasures being sold on the black market. Our host last evening, Mr. Franz Meyer, was one of these collectors."

"So, Meyer has the chalice?"

"Meyer had a beautiful porcelain vase. He was quite fond of it. If he had realized its true value, he might have protected it better. As it was, he paid a substantial sum for the piece and he wasn't pleased when he spotted one of his guests climbing out a window with the vase secured under her arm."

"Was that you? Did you steal the vase? But I don't understand —what does the vase have to do with the chalice?"

"The vase was constructed about the chalice. In this way, the Order of the Chalice thought they might protect their treasure. I threw the vase out the window and shattered it. Mr. Meyer was not happy. The vase was worthless to me—I only wanted what was inside."

"The chalice?" Trixie's eyes brightened and she smiled slyly. She reached across to grab her satchel and stroked the bag as if it were a kitten.

"To some."

"What do you mean? Can I see it?" Trixie slowly unbuckled the straps of her leather satchel and reached inside. She pulled out what appeared to be a large rock and held it for me to admire."

"I don't know. Can you?" I closed my eyes and looked again. All I saw was a rock. In the distance, coming from the sea, I heard the unmistakable piping of a bosun's whistle. Trixie pulled a whistle from her pocket and responded to the call with a series of whistles. "I'm afraid our time is short, mon amour." Trixie replaced the rock in the satchel.

"Wait, that's it?" Trixie looked at me, her eyes watering up.

"No, my dearest; not quite. Permettez-moi le plaisir d'un baiser."

"What?"

"Allow me the pleasure of a kiss." Trixie slid off the rock and reached out both her hands, helping me to my feet. She pulled me in tightly and I wrapped my arms around her and we kissed. I'd never experienced anything like that in my life. We held our embrace, kissing passionately. At that moment, there were only two of us in the world. Gradually, we peeled ourselves apart, still looking into each other's eyes. I felt a tear roll down my cheek, but Trixie caught it with her finger. She reached back into her satchel and pulled out a magnificent chalice of gold. I stared in disbelief. Trixie winked and put her finger to her lips to hush me, saving me the embarrassment of fumbling for words. None were necessary. She scampered across the rocky beach to where the sea met the land and lowered the cup into the sea, filling it with water. A voice cried out, in French, as a small rowboat appeared out of the fog, slowly making its way to the shoreline. Trixie responded, "Bienvenu!" as she was returning to me with the chalice. Clasped in both hands, she offered the chalice to me, silently bidding me to take a sip. I prepared myself for the salty taste of the sea but, instead, my palate was blessed by a sweet and indescribably divine flavor, unlike anything I had ever tasted before. Instinctively, I knew that one sip was all I should ingest. To sample any more would be folly. I handed the chalice back to Trixie. She dipped her slender finger into the water and then formed a cross upon my forehead with the wet finger. I stood there, motionless. Trixie returned to the water's edge and emptied the remaining contents of the chalice into the sea before replacing the vessel within the satchel. The rowboat reached the shore and the two oarsmen pulled the boat up onto the beach. Trixie approached the men and handed the satchel to the fella with a prodigious mustache. She then returned for what I knew would be our final goodbyes.

"You're leaving now, aren't you? I swear, I'd die a thousand times over for you, Trixie. You know that, right? If I thought it would help, I'd beg you to stay. I've never met a gal as classy as you and if you get on that boat... if you get on that boat, my heart's just going to break and there's nothing that'll ever fix it." Trixie embraced me and we kissed again.

"I'm taking the chalice home, Jimmy. I can't take you with me. Know that I love you. I always will. You weren't an accomplice, a pilot for hire, or a means to an end. You are a soulmate." Trixie gently wiped a tear from my face, and I wiped one from hers. She slowly backed away, her eyes never leaving me as she moved toward the boat. Once she was seated, her comrades pushed the boat back into the surf and pulled themselves aboard. They lifted the oars and began to row against the tide. From the boat, Trixie shouted, "Bravo pour le capitaine!" Her comrades responded with a rousing "Bravo pour le capitaine!" I watched in anguish, straining for every last moment of visual contact with Trixie Beauchamp. I yelled into the fog.

"Hey, Trixie, you never told me the name of the girl in your story—the girl who went with the pilgrims!" Trixie's reply found me through the fog.

"Beatrice. Her name was Beatrice."

"Will I ever see you again, Trixie?" There was silence; a painful silence.

"Oui, mon capitaine. Look for the white lily. Au revoir, for now, my love." Her voice was now barely audible. There was no point in shouting back. Au revoir, dearest friend.

Author's Note:

I found this strange tale in an old cedar chest in my aunt's attic. After her passing, I was assigned the unenviable task of settling her estate. There was a little note attached claiming that the pages were torn from the diary of one James Douglas. Beneath the yellowing pages from the diary, I discovered a small notebook, apparently belonging to my aunt. Within the partially filled notebook were dozens of cryptic scribbled notes along with some additional details regarding the origin of the story in question.

After Mr. Douglas abandoned his Manhattan apartment, for reasons unknown, the landlord collected what little remained to either sell or discard. Assessing the two diary volumes he came upon as having no value, he tossed them in the trash bin. Fortunately, his wife, who was there assisting in the purge, appraised the books differently. She chastised her husband and moved quickly to recover them from the garbage. She was very curious about the stranger in the leather flying jacket who came and went but said very little. The diary merited further investigation. She retained them for several weeks but, being a superstitious man, her husband finally insisted that they be thrown away. He thought it was bad luck to keep the journals of a dead man. While there was absolutely no indication that their former tenant had met his demise, his wife consented . . . but not before carefully removing a number of pages describing the strange relationship between Mr. Douglas and a mysterious flapper girl who he met one winter's eve in the City. Those pages were carefully preserved over the years in my aunt's chest of special memories until they found their way into my hands. Aunt Sally always was a sucker for a good love story. I enjoyed the story but I was left unsatisfied by the abrupt ending and unanswered questions.

I carefully reviewed the notes my aunt had made in her notebook. Most had no meaning to me but my curiosity was peaked by references to several small towns in the northeast of France. The connection to the story was not clear. Like a slow-burning candle, the story dimly lit a corner of my mind, all but forgotten but never extinguished. For me, the tale was interesting but not compelling.

I had become so focused on developing my career that I had little room for flights of fancy or far-fetched tales of romance. I was content to walk the here and now and leave the daydreaming for those with less drive to succeed. I was a fool. I soon discovered that promotions and professional accolades brought me little joy. There was something missing. When an opportunity for a business venture in the north of France was briefed at the executive round-table, I felt strangely compelled to volunteer to lead the team. Business negotiations were successfully concluded, after a week of meetings, and I released my team to return to the U.S. while I remained. Officially, I was enjoying several days of vacation to celebrate our successes in closing a multimillion-dollar deal with the French automotive company we'd been courting. My true purpose was so far out of character that I doubted my own intentions. With my aunt's well-worn notebook in hand, I would attempt to complete a sentimental journey that she, sadly, never had the resources to embark upon. And thus, I found myself dreamily staring out the window of a passenger train in the north of France.

I was pleased to have the entire row of seats to myself. It's interesting now to recall the frustration I felt when, at the very next stop, I had to stand and step into the aisle so that an older gentleman could join me in what I inappropriately assumed was my row. It wasn't long before I humbly conceded that it was our row. No, that's not it either. I was a guest in his row.

The old man greeted me warmly. His English was fairly good. I nodded and responded, reflexively. I regretted not having a paper to read—burying my head in a copy of the Wall Street Journal was a time-honored tradition employed by those who had no desire to interact with the humanity surrounding them. Instead, I pulled my aunt's notebook from my overcoat pocket and studied the notes. The old man seemed fascinated by the little book and he was not going to give me an easy out. He introduced himself as François and inquired as to the contents of the notebook and the purpose of my travel. It's funny how you can talk to a stranger, someone you know you'll never see again, and share things that you might never share with those closest to you. As I told the tale of Captain Douglas and Miss Beauchamp, his eyes lit up. He seemed to be hanging on every word. François was a diminutive French gentleman with a heart so large I'm surprised his tiny frame could bear the load. I didn't realize it at the time but he was about to become part of my strange pilgrimage.

After a considerable period of silence, François looked upward and recited some form of prayer, in French. He then rested his hand upon my shoulder and told me that it was fate that brought us together. I was skeptical. My doubt soon faded as he shared that he was familiar with the story, albeit he'd heard it told from a different perspective. He explained how the tale was relayed to him by a monk he met at a hospital while being treated for a life-threatening illness, a number of years ago. The doctors called his recovery nothing short of miraculous. François insisted the story had given him the will to live. He became obsessed with the tale and had spent many years investigating the story. That I should meet a man on a train in northern France who shared my interest in an otherwise unknown love story was beyond fascinating. Perhaps we might assist one another on our quests? I began to pick the old man's brain for every scrap of information he had about the two protagonists—I had to know more. What became of Captain Jimmy Douglas? Did he ever see Trixie again? What became of the mysterious chalice? Was it the Holy Grail or, perhaps, another otherworldly vessel? With no shortage of time on our journey, François went on to tell the remainder of the story; so much as was told to him.

After Trixie disappeared into the fog, Jimmy remained at the beach and was greeted by a sunrise of incredible beauty. As he returned to the path between the trees, he found that he no longer had the need for his walking stick. The pain in his legs was gone. He kept the stick, all the same, as it was a gift from his beloved Trixie. After a good thirty minutes of hiking, Jimmy found a road and eventually hitched a ride to the nearest bus station where he was able to work his return to New York. While sliding his bus ticket into the pocket of his flight jacket, he was shocked to discover a large stash of hundred-dollar bills—a secret gift from Trixie to help him get by. With renewed confidence and a sense of purpose, he landed a good job working at a children's hospital in New York City. There were lean times, especially during the Great Depression, but he managed to scrape by and did what he could to help others get through the many challenges in their lives. The years passed but Jimmy never stopped looking. Every time he saw a white lily, he stopped and thought of Trixie. He followed signs and portents; most leading nowhere—but it didn't seem to matter. So long as he was thinking of Trixie, he was happy. Ever so thrifty, Captain Douglas was saving every nickel so that he might, some-day, take a trip to France. Though the years passed, he never lost hope that he might be reunited with Miss Beauchamp. He wondered if she thought of him. When the Second World War wreaked death and destruction across much of the globe, Jimmy prayed and prayed hard. He prayed for an end to war and he prayed that Trixie would come through it, unharmed. And all the money he'd been saving—he gave it all away to charities supporting the countless orphans of the war.

The details of Jimmy's post-war life were sketchier. François claims to have spoken to a woman who lived in his apartment and who frequently dropped off Jimmy's mail. She told of a perfumed letter that arrived one day—it came in a white linen envelope with a lily embossed upon the exterior. There was no return address on the letter. Since she'd never seen Jimmy bringing women to his apartment and never knew him to date, it got her attention. Within days, he was gone. He paid a month's rent in advance and simply walked out the door. After that point, according to François, the trail went cold. No one in New York ever heard from Jimmy Douglas again. Not only that, but no one he interviewed had ever seen Jimmy show any symptoms of Post-Traumatic Stress Disorder, or "Shell Shock," as they called it back in the day. Perhaps the magic waters of the chalice had cured that, as well? It was a lovely thought.

I was fascinated by the story and, like my new friend, François, hoped that, somehow, things worked out for Trixie and Jimmy. I like happy endings. I was happy to leave it there. François drifted off to sleep and I occasionally readjusted his blanket so that it wouldn't fall to the floor. Sweet man. My mind drifted to wonderful places. The story of Trixie and Jimmy filled my thoughts. When our train stopped at a small town, just outside of Lille, I was startled to see a white lily upon the station sign. My heart raced. My rational brain told me to keep my seat; my destination was still over an hour away. My heart got the better of me. I stood and pulled my bag off the rack above the seats and made my way down the aisle. As I watched the train pull away, I began to wonder what I had gotten myself into. I didn't speak French and I knew absolutely nothing about the town. Eventually, I found lodging in a Bed and Breakfast and asked the proprietor if they were familiar with any ruined abbeys in the vicinity. Apparently, there were several. The next morning, I rented a bicycle and began my excursion. I must have biked nearly a hundred and fifty miles between the six sites I investigated before I saw the light. Bursting forth from a rift in the clouded sky, a ray of hope-inspiring sunlight seemed to be illuminating a wooded area in the distance. My legs were tired but I pedaled furiously toward the spot. Pulling my bicycle off the road and leaning it against a tree, I worked my way inward through the woods. It was there, in an overgrown clearing, that I saw the ruins of what appeared to be a very old abbey. I was investigating several graves marked with stone slabs when I nearly jumped out of my skin, startled by a voice coming from behind me. It was François, wrapped in the blanket that I had been readjusting while he slept. "I thought I might find you here," he said. "May I join you?" I thought to ask him any number of the hundred questions that were dancing around in my head but my heart won over my rational brain, yet again, and I merely thanked him for his companionship. He followed me as I walked, inspecting each marker. I was trying to make out the worn name on one stone when François gently placed his hand on my shoulder. "Perhaps you might try looking over there," he said. He pointed to an area away from the foundation of the abbey that appeared as a brilliant white patch amidst the lush green grass. I walked toward the spot and was astonished to see a garden of white lilies. A single stone slab, made of white marble, stood apart from any of the other markers at the site. "James M. Douglas and Beatrice B. Douglas." The remainder was in French. I looked to François for assistance with the translation. "Bound forever in love and free to fly upon wings of joy, uplifted by unbreakable faith." Beautiful. As I walked around the grave, I stumbled, nearly tripping over another stone hidden within the vegetation. I cleared the area to discover a marble block with a lily depicted, in relief, upon the top. I looked back at François. He said nothing but a slight smile made an appearance upon his aged face. I carefully replaced the concealing cover and stepped back. François nodded in approval. We both stood there for a while, absorbing what I can only describe as "the magic" of the moment. Eventually, we returned to the road. François flagged down a passing van and, after some negotiating in French, convinced the driver to take me and my bicycle back to town. François remained. We waved farewell as my van pulled away from the site.

I don't know how much of François' story is true. I'll never know if the events described in Captain Douglas' diary occurred as he described. The truth is often elusive. I do know that I'm prepared to take it all on faith. I will likely never see François again but I owe him a debt of gratitude just as I owe my aunt, and James and Trixie Douglas. I owe them all for opening my heart to a beautiful world I have never known; one I shall never part from. What of the abbey? you ask. I never went back. I don't plan to. I don't need to. It'll be there, just where it's meant to be. And, as for what secrets lay hidden beneath the Lily Stone—well, that's for you to decide.

David Lange was born and grew up on Long Island, New York. A graduate of the United States Air Force Academy, he served for 30 years as an Active Duty officer in the United States Air Force before retiring in 2018. Colonel Lange is a decorated combat veteran, and flew numerous combat, combat support, and humanitarian relief missions during his career. He was awarded the prestigious Institute of Navigation Superior Achievement Award in recognition of his life-long accomplishments as a practicing navigator. David loves sharing stories of hope and inspiration and, in 2020, he published his memoir, "Quest: My Journey Through La Mancha."

www.davidlangequest.com

2

AN ACT OF SENSELESSNESS

SHEVAUN CAVANAUGH KASTL

I

It was well after 3 AM when Lou Mansfield and Wyatt Peterson left the party. The sounds of drunken debauchery, shrieks of terror, and squeals of ghoulish delight echoed in their wake. Wyatt couldn't help but look back at the house, a gaudy neon spectacle still roaring with Halloween fun. He would have stayed. He was only a *little* drunk. Five beers he'd had. Maybe six. Was it seven? Surely not...

Lou yanked his arm with more than a little force and he stumbled forward and nearly into a zombified Michael Jackson strutting past with Princess Leia on his arm.

"Jeez, Lou! I nearly bit the ground!" But Lou wasn't having it. "You're schnockered!" she said. "And it's no wonder after those two shotsa tequila!" Wyatt rubbed the arm of his Tony Montana pinstriped suit sheepishly. He'd forgotten about the shots.

"Well, are ya coming, or do I hafta drive myself home?" Lou was at the car already, bobbing her bleached blonde and pink head impatiently and glaring at Wyatt as he shuffled reluctantly away from the house toward the yellow Buick Skyhawk he'd managed to squeeze between a rusty Ford pickup and a sleek, smokey-grey Firebird, both of whose owners were still inside, enjoying the holiday hoopla. "Oh for Pete's sake!" he muttered under his breath. "What's that now?" Her tone was brittle, like the cold that was stinging his cheeks. Lou was a master of polite disdain. They'd been dating for over a year and, though he surely loved her, sometimes he thought about how she might die. And when.

The fuzzy warmth of intoxication was wearing off quickly as Wyatt fished the keys out of his back pocket and fumbled with the lock. His fingers were already numb from the cold and his eyes were watering. Lou continued to bob. "Will ya hurry up? I can't feel my feet!" Wyatt puffed out a cloud of hot air. "Maybe you shoulda considered the weather before dressing up in fishnets and a see-through shirt."

He thought it, but didn't dare say it. Lou was obsessed with Madonna. "Lucky Star" was practically her anthem, and any critique would land about as well as a tornado on any day but Wednesday.

"Will ya just... just gimme a sec here. It's colder than a polar bear's toenail." He could feel her glower. Lou was pretty, but her lips were chronically pursed in disapproval and her wide hazel eyes were always tinged with hostility. "Oh sure. Take your time. I always thought I'd go in my sleep but I suppose freezin' to death is more dramatic."

Freezin' to death. He hadn't thought of that.

At last, Wyatt succeeded in unlocking the door and moments later the couple sped off down County Route 4. They drove in silence. Lou was too busy thawing her stiff frozen fingers in the hot air blasting from the vents to bother with banter. Wyatt was glad for it. He had a headache and his glasses were fogging up from the clash of warm air inside the car and the sub-zero temperature outside.

II

Wyatt lost all sense of time as they drove in darkness. His lids grew heavy. *Maybe it was seven beers.* He braved a glance over at Lou. She was sleeping. At least, her eyes were closed. She looked so peaceful. Angelic even. When they met fourteen months ago at the Thrifty White, he hadn't been lookin' for anything. But the minute he saw her at the photo kiosk he knew he was gonna marry Lou Mansfield and that was that.

Wyatt sighed and turned his gaze back to the road. He was so tired. And the hot air pumping through the vents was making his eyes well. Minutes passed. Each one felt longer than the last. The yellow line in the road grew bleary, and then doubled.

The sharp swerve of the car sent a jolt of alarm through Lou's body and her eyes flew open. "Jesus H. Christ, Wy! Watch the freakin' road!" Wyatt shouted back defensively. "I was watchin' the road. It just... it just came outta nowhere!" Lou's wide hazel eyes narrowed to slits, her voice pitched low and dripping with contempt. "What came outta nowhere?" Wyatt fought to get the words out. She was angry. More than angry. "A- a deer I think."

Lou scowled at the man beside her. When she met Wyatt two years ago, she thought he had potential. He was weak, sure. Anybody could tell that. And he drank too much. But what guy didn't? She could mold him. Heck, she could do anything she set her mind to. Only... She didn't have the patience. Two long years. Too long.

"Pull over," she said. It was very matter-of-fact and caught Wyatt off-guard. "What?" he stammered. She repeated the declaration at an even lower decibel, accentuating each word with an inflection that could cut glass. "I said, pull over, Wyatt Peterson." Wyatt rolled his weary eyes and steered the car over to the side of the road. He watched in disbelief as Lou got out, pulled her coat tight, and slammed the door.

"Oh fer... It was a deer!" he called out. But if she heard him, she didn't show it. Lou stomped off into the frigid night, alone. Fishnets be damned.

Wyatt couldn't be sure how long he sat there. Exhaustion had taken hold of his body and the heat lulled him into a kind of trance. He knew he had to go after her. That much was clear. Only...

III

Lou couldn't see her hands, but she knew they were frozen, even with mitts. She should go back. She'd made her point. But something deep inside her refused to turn around. She hadn't been walking that long. Ten minutes? Fifteen, maybe? It was hard to know. "No good, waste of time, drunk." She huffed.

Her thoughts wandered back to Jimmy Anderson–her ex-boyfriend and High School sweetheart. She shoulda stuck with Jimmy. He had nothin' upstairs but he knew how to treat a lady. Lou was so engrossed in thoughts of "What if" she almost didn't realize it wasn't nearly so dark. Was the sun coming up?

IV

Wyatt strained his eyes for any sign of Lou as he drove. She couldn't have got that far on foot. He glanced at the clock. 3:45am.

When did they leave the party? As the seconds passed, Wyatt started to panic. *It's too cold. She'll freeze.*

He stepped on the gas.

It happened so fast. The flash of movement, the hard impact that sent a shudder through the whole of Wyatt's body, the bits of meat and skin and blood-spatter on the windshield. He slammed on the brakes and the car swerved and skidded to a halt. Panting, trembling, Wyatt killed the engine and stepped out of the car. When he saw the body, he laughed. An inappropriate response, sure, but he was just so gosh darn relieved. "Well, whaddya know. It *was* a deer."

It was that overwhelming relief that shielded Wyatt Peterson from the trauma of killing a living thing. And it was that same relief that blinded him from the sudden, harsh glare of headlights and the loud horn of a truck moving far too fast on County Route 4.

When Wyatt hit the ground, he thought he mighta broke every bone in his body. He laid there, still as a corpse, for several minutes before one thought came to mind that dared him to move. Lou. Lou with the blonde hair and the big hazel eyes that bore into his soul. Lou, a woman who could hurl insults and a barrel of corn to boot, and in heels no less. With all his might, Wyatt dug his benumbed fingers into the frosty ground and pushed himself up.

He found his glasses a few feet away. One lens was cracked, and the frame was bent, but at least they were intact. Wyatt limped past the bloody carcass to the car and started the engine.

V

"Lou!" Wyatt slowed the car to match Lou's pace. She was

ambling along the side of the road, frozen and bone-tired, but she didn't stop. *Did she not hear him?* He rolled down the passenger side window and called out again. This time, she turned, lips still pursed in disapproval. Or was it disappointment? It didn't matter anymore. "I'm sorry Lou. Please get in the car." To his surprise, she didn't argue. No snappy retort. No anger. Something else though. She looked sad.

Wyatt was gentle as he buckled Lou in and turned the heat to full blast. "We'll getcha warmed up in no time." His smile was tender. Sincere. He almost looked like the guy she met at the Sweet Swede Candy Shoppe two years prior. Full of potential. "I hit a deer," Wyatt remarked with a clueless grin of self-satisfaction. "Yer prouda that, are ya?" she replied. The condescension had returned, but Wyatt didn't care. "Yeah, actually. I told ya. There was a deer. It wasn't the drink." Another clueless smile and he put the car in drive. It was nearly sunrise by the time they reached the Lindstrom County line.

Wyatt pulled the car over and parked, just as the sun peeked over the horizon. Lou gave him a puzzled stare. "Why're we stopping?" He took her hand in his... still so cold to the touch. "I thought we could, ya know, watch the sunrise. Together." She stared back at him blankly, opened her mouth to speak, but didn't. They sat in silence as the sun made its ascent and broke the night.

VI

The bodies of Lou Mansfield and Wyatt Peterson were found later that morning. Victims of a tragic hit and run, Chief Patrick Lawson ruled, and a horrific act of senselessness. The couple's untimely deaths made the front page of the Chisago County Press. "Investigation ongoing." But three weeks later, a Winter Storm blasted the Northern plains in one of the worst blizzards in history. A record-breaking 13 feet of snow buried the township of

Lindstrom and the investigation along with it. The story was all but forgotten, save a small citation in the town's historical archives.

"On Halloween night, 1983, Lou Mansfield and Wyatt Peterson left a friend's party on County Route 4 and sped off into the night, never to be seen alive again."

Shevaun Cavanaugh Kastl is a natural-born Storyteller. While she began as a Singer and Dancer in such professional NY stage productions as On the Town, Disney's Beauty and the Beast, and West Side Story, Shevaun later discovered her true passion - Writing and Filmmaking. Her first Short film, "Conversations With Lucifer" was honored among hundreds as one of four films to screen at the historic Grauman's Egyptian Theatre. Her second script, "The Mourning Hour" won the title of Best Screenplay at the Slugline International Short Screenplay Competition and the film went on to receive critical acclaim with top honors at The Grand Off Film Festival in Warsaw, Poland, among many other festivals.

While Shevaun continues to write for the Big Screen, she has expanded her literary portfolio to include Poetic Prose, Short Stories, and One-Act Plays. Her most recent piece "Somebody's Unicorn" was published last month in the Red Penguin Anthology "A Heart Full of Love - A Collection of Romantic Short Stories." She has now written three Feature Screenplays and is currently writing a Psychological Thriller as well as a Fantasy Novel.

3

ALIVE IN THE BASEMENT

ERIC WAYNE

In a spacious bedroom on the upstairs floor of a Greek Revival home, a wife (or what was left of her) sat by a window overlooking the property's courtyard. A stroke had rendered her unable to speak, move, or hear. What she could see with her eyes, no one could say.

A marriage of 52 years, however, had created other languages that spoke. It was this communication that kept the couple conversing, at least in the mind of her husband.

He called up to her from the base of the winding staircase.

"Hungry?" he asked. He heard no response.

"Alice, are you hungry? And will you be joining the conference downstairs?"

Seymour walked up the stairs past the portrait of the man who was the subject of today's annual symposium, John Dewey. Born in this Vermont house 150 years ago, it had been 66 years since the great man's death.

Seymour held a plate with a sandwich on it for Alice, and a glass of water.

John Dewey, the 19th century educator who would replace schoolroom memorization with modern hands-on learning, changing education forever.

John Dewey, the 19th century philosopher who was a founding father to such great movements as the NAACP and the ACLU.

Seymour stopped for a moment on the staircase and gazed at the portrait of the old educator. From the frame, Dewey appeared to look out at the viewers as if they were students about to ask a question. Since his death in 1951, the John Dewey Society had been holding annual conferences on his birthday, and today, Sunday, was the day.

At the top of the stairs, Seymour entered the bedroom he shared with his wife and found her staring out of the window at the giant pine trees in the courtyard.

"A beautiful day, is it not, Alice?" he pondered aloud.

When she did not move her head, he bent down to look at her. Her eyes were open, gazing at a blue heron that had gotten lost and was now resting on an upper extremity of one of the magnificent trees.

Seymour placed the glass of water on the windowsill.

"That bird does not look like it should be there at all!" he exclaimed, admiring its wingspan as it stretched.

He looked into Alice's eyes for comment, eyes that he could read after more than five decades of marriage. *It's a female, Seymour. I think she is building her nest on old George here. How exciting! I haven't seen the male yet. He is the one that gathers the branches, and the female arranges them. What a treat we have in store!*

But as soon as he understood Alice's words, the great bird launched from the branch and headed west toward Lake Champlain. Its black legs disappeared into its blue and white feathers. The great bird bounced in the gravity before calling its strength to even out its flight. *Such a beautiful bird, Seymour.*

From the northern windows around to the west, they watched the bird fly and then

disappear behind a neighboring home. "That wasn't a blue heron! It was a great egret, Alice!"

Same old Seymour, always the biologist. It's a blue heron to me.

"Taylor will be here for dinner, Alice." She was always excited to see their only child. He came every Sunday, sometimes bringing his wife and two teenage children.

Alice did not appear to be breathing.

He helped her into her favorite robe, because Deborah – where the hell was Deborah, anyway? – was not caregiving as she should be!

"I'm going to join the conference downstairs, Alice. Is there anything else I can get for you? Deborah, come here please!"

No, thank you. I am just going to sit here and look out at this glorious day. If I need you, I will call.

"Well, I'll be downstairs," he said, mumbling Deborah's name as he left the room.

At the base of the stairs, the long hallway that stood before him spilled forth into the front parlor. He could see people sitting in chairs and hear the soft rumble of words coming from a speaker who was out of his view.

As Seymour entered the room, he leaned his weight against the doorframe. The attention of everyone in the room was toward the speaker. He wore round spectacles, and the flaps of his wide-collared shirt sprung out from his suit. It was finely tailored in Edwardian style and quite dapper. Seymour could not focus on his face. From where he stood in the back of the room, he could only make out the backs of the attendees' heads.

Even though the man at the podium spoke in a monotone voice, the crowd listened intently to every word. A man seated directly in front of Seymour (whose attire spoke of a clergyman) chose a random moment for a query.

"Mr. Dewey," the man began in a confident, southern drawl, "you put farthe that education in dis 'ere country should be based on, what choo call 'sperimention and hands-on activity, yet the lack of 'ligious faith in this cahntry, and indeed da worl', is what is truly lackin', Mistah Dewey. Sawly lackin'! Fact is, it seems to me that these two natural 'ccurances are in conflict with one another."

The man turned his attention away from the speaker and addressed the crowd with open arms.

"That not so, ladies and gentlemen?" A fly buzzed around his head.

John Dewey breathed in deeply and adjusted the spectacles on his face.

"Any trained observer of nature can answer your question, Sir. Perhaps in our company today we may be so lucky as to have a biologist." He looked up toward Seymour. "To the biologist, I ask, does there exist in the natural world two opposing forces that ultimately combine to serve one another?"

Seymour raised a lazy hand to the question, but simultaneously a hand shot up from another man seated nearby.

Seymour seized the moment, "Well, if it helps," he began in a voice loud enough for all to hear, "Alice and I were not ten minutes ago observing a large bird on the grounds. She was convinced it was a blue heron, while I could plainly see it was a great egret. The two species collaborate in nature to control the rodent problem along the shores of Lake Champlain."

No one responded or reacted to Seymour's statement, and the sound of a military jet now thundered overhead, shaking the house. No one in the room seemed to notice its deafening roar.

The clergyman seated in front of Seymour took the moment to elaborate.

"Mr. Dewey, I adhere to the science of our natural world as created by God. As a pragmatist...."

"It is the foundation of my studies, Mr...."

"McKain. Pastor Kevin McKain, at your service." He dipped his top hat toward the speaker.

Out of the paned window, Seymour watched as a delivery driver headed up the walkway with a package. The man tapped on his handheld device, looked up at the house, and placed the box on the porch. No one else seemed to notice.

"Thank you, Mr. McKain. Indeed, I profess that students would be better served by less memorization of fact. Instead, we should emphasize participation in learning experiments that bring out students' individual interests."

The clergyman brought forth a Bible from under his frock and held it above his head like a winning lottery ticket. "So, you profess that we should in fact build academic laboratories where students dilly dally about instead of realizing the tried and true word of God?" he exclaimed, his face flushed.

"The self is not something ready-made," the speaker continued. "It is something in continuous formation through choice of action," he said.

The clergyman stood up in a violent gesture. "I have a sermon to give," he declared. Still, no heads turned toward him. He brushed past Seymour and disappeared down the hallway toward the cellar door, which oddly cracked open as the man approached. The man abruptly stopped halfway down the hall and slowly turned toward Seymour.

Shockingly, the man had only the bare relics of a face, his grey skin stuck to his bones like puddy to a brittle surface. Where there should have been eyes, there were only holes. Where there should have been a human hand, there were only frail remnants. As Seymour watched in astonishment, what appeared to be a great rushing wind sucked the man backwards into the basement. The door slammed shut behind him.

Incredulous, Seymour turned toward the front of the room where the conference continued. John Dewey raised his palms in question.

"This is an open forum," he stated plainly. "Only ordinary citizens know what is best for them."

Now Seymour began to study what he could see of the attendees around the room. There were both men and women and their clothes hung loosely and without form over their bones. A woman, adorning a flower-pot hat, wore puffy sleeves that drooped over grey shoulders.

Suddenly the phone rang, making a shrill noise, and repeated. Seymour ducked into the hallway and called out for the caregiver.

"Deborah! Answer the phone!"

The speaker continued. "Imagine, my friends, a school that is not a school at all, but a

hands-on learning center. Where children not only learn how soil cultivates growth, but actually grow the food themselves."

Riiing! Riiing!

Seymour ran to the kitchen, where he answered the phone in a huffed gasp.

"Hello!" It came out as a statement.

"Dad?"

"Hello?"

"Dad, it's Taylor."

"Dad, how's everything going? I should be there in a half hour. Do you need me to pick up anything special from the store?"

"Doing fine, fine, Boy."

No one spoke.

"Can I speak to Deborah?"

Seymour stared at a mason jar of herbal tea. His throat was sore. He turned on the gas burner, and it spurred on after a few seconds. Seymour looked around for the kettle.

"No, no actually." He held the phone to his chest. "Deborah! Deborah! Come here!"

"Dad, where is Deborah?"

"I don't know. I have not seen her all day." He held the phone out from his body.

"Deborah!" he called. "Deborah!" He held the phone back up to his ear.

"Who is helping you, Dad?" Taylor asked.

"We are having a conference here today. I'm fine."

"Conference?"

"Yes, and I need to get back to it."

There was no response.

"Dad, are you there?"

"Yes, I'm here Boy! I am going to go check on your Mother."

"Dad, where is Deborah? What is wrong with Mom?"

Seymour held the phone to his chest. Where was Deborah? He tried to remember. She was not there because...ah, now he remembered. He had caught Deborah stealing his wallet from the top drawer of his bureau a couple of days ago.

"You stole my wallet! Get out of this house!" he had said to her. "Leave right now, you wretched...THIEF!"

"Taylor says that I should hold onto your wallet for you," she had said in a sing-song

Bahamian accent. "It is safe here in my bag. I will not be spoken to in that manner, Mr. Seymour. Goodbye." She handed over the wallet, gathered her belongings, and left.

"Deborah! Deborah! Come back here! I'm sorry," he called out. Only the great pine trees were there to hear his words.

"Dad? Are you there? I'll be there in a half hour."

Seymour placed the phone down, missing the cradle that was next to the lit pilot. There was still no kettle on. He exited the kitchen and rejoined the conference.

"We are engaged right now in a great public experiment," John Dewey continued. "The stark contrasts between William Jennings Bryan and William McKinley in the upcoming election are perhaps the greatest this country has seen in its grand 100-year history."

The suffragists in the room smiled, and again the tension became its own elephant. The woman with the flower-pot hat sat up straight. "Indeed, Professor. Two more old men to decide for all women," she said. It came out as a joke, a question and a statement. The sound of female laughter filled the crowded room.

A man who was well-known in the railroad circles of Burlington took his turn to speak up.

"It is not that the current system disqualifies women from voting."

His voice was high pitched, and he spoke as if he were an instructor to those of lesser intellect.

"In any household, Madam, a man and a woman discuss the issues, and the man merely registers the opinion of both."

He appealed to the audience with his logic.

A debate ensued as Seymour observed from his perch by the doorframe. Another military jet screamed across the sky, drowning out the speaker, but he neither raised his voice nor seemed phased by the deafening sound that shook the house.

A smell began to permeate the room, horrible and stinging. Seymour followed the stench into the kitchen.

The stove burner was spitting out its blue flame, and someone, somehow, had left the phone receiver directly on the raw flame. A black mound of melting plastic was cooking on the flame, and the sight was so odd and fascinating that Seymour could not break his gaze from it. In the front parlor, he heard the murmur of the ongoing social debate.

"What will be next for women? Females soldiers in the Spanish American War?"

Seymour stood still and watched the angry flame grow. Its stain began to paint the ceiling in dripping black soot.

"Deborah! Deborah!" he called out. He realized that he had hardly dressed this morning, and his pajama bottoms were now soiled from his panic.

"Fire! Fire! There's a fire!"

He grabbed a towel Deborah had left in an unfolded laundry pile in the pantry. He ran over to the flames and began patting the source. He left the towel on the flame, exited the kitchen, and ran into the parlor.

"Fire! Fire! I say, there's a fire!" he screamed.

The woman in the flower-pot hat ignored him and continued.

"There can be no democracy without the full participation of its citizens, and by citizens I mean WOMEN!"

She spoke in the tone of someone who is no longer interested in giving an opinion, but rather stating facts.

The railroad man again addressed the woman. "Then perhaps, Madam, you should have no objection to enlisting your daughters to fight in the Indian territory." The remark drew gasps from some and stifled laughter from others.

"People, please! All of you, GET OUT OF THE HOUSE!"

The woman addressed her accuser.

"Be careful Sir, because Manifest Destiny has a way of sneaking into your own house," she hissed.

Now Seymour began to shout louder. The thick smoke was starting to permeate the front room.

"FIRE!"

Alice.

Alone upstairs.

"Everyone, please save yourselves! LEAVE THIS HOUSE!" he screamed and ran into the hallway, passing the closed basement door through which the clergyman had been swept downward.

From the staircase, the portrait of John Dewey looked down at him. The man sat in his wingback chair. Papers spilled from his hands. The flaps of his shirt sprung out.

Murmurs from the front room continued.

"As we enter the 20th century, we need to envision a planning society where workers and consumers would participate in decisions affecting their lives and communities."

Thick smoke was now beginning to circulate in the hallway and make its way up the stairs.

Alarms sounded.

Answer the phone!

No, these alarms were louder and even more shrill.

"Alice! Alice! There's a fire! I'm coming, Alice!"

He ran back into the kitchen and grabbed a shirt from the folded laundry. On the stove, the towel was now fully aflame and what was once the phone was oozing burnt plastic onto the floor. He ran over to the stove and switched the burner off, but the dials started turning on their own in confusing circles. Another burner hissed and lit up. Again, Seymour ran out of the kitchen.

He began to ascend the stairs again, struggling to catch his breath. He stopped and rested on the ballister which snaked its way up out of sight toward the second floor. He crashed on the third step and smacked his face. He felt warm blood emit from his eye.

"Alice, I'm coming! We need to get out of the house!" He gasped for air.

Seymour, what is that smell? What is that smell? Please, I can't walk. The stroke, Seymour! Remember, I cannot move, Seymour.

"Education, women's rights, unions...it all must evolve with our society, or our great melting pot will disintegrate before our eyes."

Seymour, help me.

"Please, everyone leave. There's a fire. Deborah! DEB-O-RAH!"

Help me Seymour.

"This annual meeting is now adjourned. Ladies and gentlemen, this debate is far from over. It will rage on. Until next year!"

Seymour lay on the stairs and struggled to open his eyes. He glimpsed down the hallway toward the conference now adjourning. As he watched, a comet-like ball of wind began to form in the parlor. Slowly at first, and then picking up speed, it appeared to suck up all the souls in attendance, whooshing them into a blinding whirlwind of faces, limbs, clothing, and strewn papers.

Having inhaled its meal, it started to barrel down the hallway toward Seymour. As it approached the basement door, the orifice began to slowly open. The mysterious sphere then paused for a moment as if to digest, and the door slammed shut with a satisfactory bang.

"I am...coming, Alice. I am...coming for you!" Choking.

Husband, there is thick smoke all around me.

Seymour struggled to gain his footing as the blaring alarm rang out, but found that he only fell deeper into a contorted position on the stairs. The fire continued to rage on.

Eric Wayne is the author of many short stories. His debut novel, The Visitor is scheduled for publication in 2021. He lives in Burlington, Vermont.

4

PERFECT PAIR

AMANDA MONTONI

Loretta glanced out at the hidden audience. It was dark. She only saw the silhouettes of the bodies in the first row sitting with their hands clutching their brandies upon the small round tables that filled the short-ceilinged square room. The stage lights illuminated the puffs of hidden smoke coming from gentlemen's Brazilian cigars. Once the puffs left the trail of light, they disappeared into thin air, just like the audience that sat in front of her each night. Just like the people in her life. It was dark and hazy from the cigar smoke. No one could completely see each other or the cleverly chosen hangings on the wall. They were all tinted masses perfectly happy under the concrete, grinning among the subway lines. Even though everyone was breathing the exact same smoke-filled air, it was a room full of strangers. A room of the unknown.

Every night at The Swanky Owl brought a different kind of tone. Some nights at the jazz club would be pure bliss, like a familiar major chord on the piano accompanied by a gracious audience and their applause. Their claps took on a song of their own. The sounds of different sized palms coming together vibrated and ricocheted a melody through the room so powerful, Loretta swore she saw the low ceilings start to shake. For a minute or two, she felt seen. On the good nights, she would walk home with a new confidence that stayed with her through the dark into the next morning.

Those nights she felt free. Free from the clutches of her past. Free from the clutches of her present. You see, Loretta was a girl trapped in the tight grip of sticky fingertips. Fingers that could never and would never be able to glide through the keys on a piano. Fingers that on nights like the good ones, she felt as if she could escape from them, until they stick her right back into their false hope-filled prints.

Her father decided alcohol was more lovable than she, and, ironically, she entertained those starry-eyed romancers for the poison every night. Bill. That was his name. She dare not speak it. The slaps on her face burn on her skin again. The hand covering her mouth to keep her screams from being heard creeps up from under her blankets. The echoes of being called useless, untalented, and unwanted echo off of the cinderblock walls of her dreams. On the good nights, she reminds herself that she got out of that lousy room her father called a home.

Then, there's Stan. The man she calls her fella. He wasn't all that bad, to begin with, but, as time passed, and since Stan is an important man at the club, let's just say if she even thinks about leaving the club or him, something bad will happen.

The good nights made her forget about Stan and his gaslighting ways. She felt at peace walking around the street-lit sidewalks all alone. She looked at the night sky and it reminded her that there is a whole world out there. The world is not the club. The world is not Manhattan. The world is a wonder to be discovered and Loretta wanted to drop a line to whomever it was that took care of it. So, she wished upon stars. She would take hours walking home when she only lived a couple of blocks away. Sometimes she would walk until the sun rose. On those mornings, she walked to the nearest coffee joint, grabbed herself a cup, sat on a bench, and watched as Manhattan slowly trickled its eyes open.

Lately, the nights for Loretta have felt flat. There were still the crowds that praised her, but it seemed that the nights she once knew have taken a step down from the adrenaline-pumping wonder she missed so dearly. There were times when Loretta felt like the nights were just about there, the way they used to be, but they always seemed to miss the spark.

Then, there were other nights. Ones of trouble. The kind of trouble that makes wild souls of good people and tomorrow unattainable. Like a minor chord that creeps up to the surface, and demolishes all of the hope left in a person. Yet, every night patrons sat at those small round tables, clutched their brandies, and breathed the same puffs of smoke from gentlemen's cigars like nothing ever happened on those nights. They seemed accustomed to them, or like they didn't exist.

When Loretta looked out at that hidden audience, she realized she knew them like herself. They were also caught in the trap, knowing they could be so much more. They were just below the mark, like she was. Flat.

The nights at The Swanky Owl are different and yet, they are all the same. How could everything around her be so different and alike at the same time? Loretta saw the same silhouetted bodies, the same stage lights that illuminated her, the same wonder that filled the room, and made a wish. She wished if, for just one night, things could be different.

However, as she played the black baby grand on the tiny 6-foot-wide stage, she didn't want to be anywhere else. This place was her home because it had the piano, and the piano was her heart and soul. Her fingers glazed upon the ivory keys with a finesse not suited for her 23-year-old self. She was beyond her years and carried herself with a stature of matureness that suggested strength, but when she smiled, it was as if she had the soul of a joyful little girl.

Children are lucky. They don't see the badness of the world. Take one look at one smiling, and an adult will instantly forget the thorn-covered vines tangled around their lives. Loretta's smile brought people in with one look. Her hovered innocence and goodness intrigued them. She laughed with them. She enjoyed them. She longed for the company, but her matureness never let people all the way in. She knew better than to trust the people she loved, and the people she didn't want to know.

When Loretta performed, all that consumed her was the black baby grand. The small stage beneath her feet disappeared. Then the audience with the cigar-filled air and the clinks of brandy-filled glasses did. So did the murmur of empty and hopeful hearts. Like looking at a child smiling, the badness of the world disappeared. The world itself disappeared. When she played, all was quiet except for the melody she poured every last inch of herself into. The music was the only one she allowed in completely.

Whistles and applause flooded the room when she took her bow. From her jazzy and jumpy melodies, those empty and hope-filled hearts became ones full of restored faith. For a moment, those hearts now beat to the drum of belief. They believed in happiness, in goodness, in the world. They believed in wishes. Most importantly, they believed in themselves. Loretta made the world a better place, even if it was only for an hour or so in the basement of a restaurant among the subway system.

The warmth from the lights upon Loretta's face was the warmth she had been missing. For one moment each night, she felt complete. She glowed. For one second out of her day, she felt the dreaded four-letter word, Hope. She needed this second to keep her going. If there is no hope, then what's the point of living?

There was only one person she wanted to see. So far, there was no sight of him. He was supposed to be at The Swanky Owl the entire week, but he was nowhere to be found, and it didn't help that she had no idea what this cat looked like. He was supposed to save her, to change her life. In the second it took for hope to fill her heart, it took just as quickly to be taken away. She should've known better. Her life was full of disappointments.

She swirled her way through the crowd as they stopped to praise her. Loretta thanked them with a gentle, grateful smile, but all the while she prayed the next person she saw would be Mr. Cowl.

"Here's your cut for the night, kid. You're the cat's meow."

The club owner wasn't Mr. Cowl, but at least she got paid. She looked up at the club owner on the other side of the bar. Her eyes were like a cigarette lighter that wouldn't work. A spark was in them, but she tried her damnedest to exterminate her optimism before she asked the question on her mind.

"I'm sorry, Retty. I haven't seen him," Joe said while wiping down the bar countertop as if he could read Loretta's thoughts.

Joe refused to be called "Mr. Russo." He was the kind of man who always said that "Mr. Russo" was his father. Now in his mid-fifties, he is a well-respected father figure. He took Loretta in when she was just 16 after she ran away from home. Joe was the closest thing to a parent Loretta ever had.

"Thanks, Joe," she said, taking a seat at the bar. He gave Loretta her usual after-show drink, a water with lemon. No giggle water for her. She never touched the stuff.

"Maybe he'll make it tomorrow night," Joe said as he tried to lift Loretta's spirits, and placed her complimentary after-show meal in front of her. Meatloaf and potatoes were on the menu tonight. Loretta took a sip of her lemon water.

"He's an honest man for a producer, believe it or not. He'll come."

"Let's hope so," Loretta said while hope quickly left her.

Suddenly, there was a loud crash of glass hitting a wall on the other side of the speakeasy. Shouts and thuds filled the room. A crowd started to form. When fights started to break out at The Swanky Owl, that's when you knew the brandies have settled in. Joe calmly motioned with one finger to Tiny, a guy hired just for this kind of stuff so as to avoid the police. His name may be small, but his stature says otherwise. He took his broad build slowly over to the crowd, which was so in awe of his presence, they parted to make a path for him. Tiny picked up the two men who were wrestling on the floor with such ease it looked as if they weighed no more than a football combined. He pulled them up by the shirts on their backs, one in each hand. The crowd's collective glance followed Tiny across the room in silence. The two men were too spifflicated to notice they were magically lifted from the floor by the effortless giant and continued to swing at each other, missing. Loretta watched as Tiny and the little levitating tough guys disappeared up the stairwell. The crowd began to disperse and the white noise of people enjoying themselves once again became the soundtrack of the basement.

SLAM. Her trance was shattered.

A man. She knew it was a man because of the manner of his hand, slammed his fist on the table.

"May I say that you play absolutely beautifully?" he said.

The slam sent her lemon water and meal hovering over the table for a moment. For just one second, she felt like the little levitating tough guys, except sober. She lost about a quarter of her refreshment.

"Excuse me. What do you think you're doing?" she responded. Whomever this beast of a man was, he was strong.

"Giving you a compliment," the beast said.

"More like giving me a heart attack," she retorted.

The man extended the hand (his left) that was just in a fist and said, "I'm Jim."

He was tall, neatly dressed in a button-down and tie, but messy. His shirt sleeves were rolled up to his elbows. His awful seafoam green and blue striped tie was loosened, and his top three buttons were undone. His chest hair popped out of his shirt like Jacks in boxes and carried his suit jacket crumpled up in his right arm while clutching a brandy. His brown hair was slicked back from sweat, and the pit stains? Oh, they were repulsive. He looked as if he had just done some heavy lifting.

She denied his handshake by taking a bite of her meatloaf. Loretta thought of telling him a fake name, but everyone already knew hers.

"Loretta."

"I know," he said with a gentle smirk.

Jim picked up the chair next to him, flipped it around using his fist-hand, and straddled it, facing Loretta.

"You know, I've seen you play many times. In fact, I've come to every one of your gigs for three weeks now and this is the first time I've had the courage to talk to you."

What a line, Loretta thought, but was he being sincere? His cheeks were red, but she couldn't exactly tell whether he was blushing, if it had something to do with why he was such a sweaty mess, or because it was alcohol-induced. Maybe it was all three.

"Well, thank you." She took his compliment.

"You're very welcome," he said with a shy smirk Loretta found surprisingly endearing.

An awkward silence filled the space between them. Loretta looked at his eyes. They were filled with black holes. The dark brown of his iris melted in with the black of his pupils. Enchanted, she felt Jim staring into her soul as if he saw all of her with one simple glance. If she wasn't careful, she could get lost in his eyes, or worse, stuck on him. Loretta held onto her lemon water for safety. Jim clutched his brandy, hoping for some liquid courage.

"Would you have a drink with me?" Jim asked her.

"Aren't I already having one with you?"

Jim looked down at her half-empty lemon water, chuckled, and said, "I have a funny feeling we'd make a perfect pair."

He flashed Loretta a giddy smile and took a sip of his drink. Loretta blushed for what felt like the first time in her entire life.

Her moment of pleasant awkwardness was quickly broken by a trapping voice.

"Hey there, Jimbo. I see ya met my gal," Stan said intimidatingly. He wrapped his meat hook around Loretta and planted an over-the-top kiss on her lips. Stan was one to mark his territory like a dog who found his favorite fire hydrant to piss all over.

"Joe, you got the payment?"

Stan was not one to discuss things in private. He loved the power he gained from putting people on the spot. Joe, on the other hand, was a man of manners.

"Stan, it's not the 13th yet. Don't you worry. You'll get your money," Joe said as respectfully as he could, hiding his boiling blood beneath the blanket of politeness.

You see, Joe took out a loan from Stan and his goons. With the cops knocking down speakeasies and arresting citizens all over the city, people were too scared to run into the looming threat of the law and their beating sticks.

"I know you're a good man, Joe. But you know I'm just the messenger. The Boss might not be as accommodating to your character," Stan threatened before he quickly directed his attention back to Jim.

"So, Jimbo. I take it everything is taken care of?" Stan said as he slid his hand down to Loretta's waist.

Loretta had absolutely no clue prior that Stan and Jim knew each other, and by the looks of it, worked together. She was quick to read rooms.

"Yes, Sir. Taken care of," Jim said like a trained guppy.

Stan quickly reflexed into the space between the civil-like and animalistic versions of himself.

"What did I tell you about calling me 'Sir', Jimmy Boy?"

Stan let his meat-hook grip loosen from Loretta's waist, morphing it into a fist at his side. Fear spread across Jim's face.

"Big Stan," Jim quickly corrected himself.

"That's better," Stan snickered as he wrapped his arm around Loretta, marking his property once again.

"Come on, doll face. How's about you and me scram?" he asked Loretta.

Trapped, she nodded in agreement and slowly made her body fit into Stan's arm as they began to leave. She took a look back at Jim and saw embarrassment coursing through his veins. But when they locked eyes, they stole a smile from each other that screamed *this is not goodbye.*

And it wasn't. Jim came to the club every night. Every night Jim and Loretta spoke over her complimentary meal, lemon water, and brandy. They stole smiles from each other and lived in false happiness, never admitting the anxiety they felt growing within their budding relationship. They didn't want to imagine all of the bad that would arrive if Stan found out about them. Joe acted as their Fairy Godfather, covering for them if Stan or one of his goons happened to drop by. Luckily, Joe gathered enough hopeless hearts at the speakeasy to pay off his loan. There were nights when Joe hid Jim underneath the bar. They would stay there and listen for hours as Loretta intelligently and oh so carefully sent Stan home without her. Joe did not want to see Loretta's wish fall like a forgotten star.

About a month later, Loretta turned 24. After her set, Jim welcomed her like he always did. If there was anyone who could get her mind away from her life, it was him.

"Happy Birthday, my love," he said as he leaned down to place a kiss upon her forehead.

Loretta noticed his unusual stature. He stood up perfectly straight with his hands behind his back.

"What are you hiding?" she said with a curious brow.

"Hiding? I'm not hiding anything," Jim said with slightly too much joy in his voice.

"What are you holding behind your back?"

"Nothing. Nothing at all," Jim said in another failed attempt to sway Loretta's intuition.

"It's my birthday present, isn't it?!"

"It's your birthday?"

"Stop lying to me!"

Jim glared up at the ceiling to play off a nonchalant whistle.

"I see right through you," she exclaimed with squinted eyelids.

"Then you can see this," Jim said as he pulled out a gold diamond bracelet from behind his back and presented it to the birthday girl.

"I knew it! Oh, It's absolutely beautiful!"

Loretta was overfilled with wonder. She has never seen anything so Ritzy before. Jim placed the bracelet onto Loretta's wrist with the gentle touch of his love.

She smiled as he said "the perfect present for part of the perfect pair."

Loretta melted. She had never come across someone as kind, compassionate, and genuine as Jim. She would marry him in a second if he asked. She threw her arms around him and kissed him like she never did before–filled with unending gratitude. A feeling she has never fully felt before him. She thanked him for everything with that one kiss.

Loretta's tune had changed. Her time with her piano on the tiny stage turned into a celebration. The piano became full of dancing keys. The audience joined them, leaving their brandies on the tables. The floor started to become shaky with Charlestons and lovers swaying joyfully. The vibration of the room was infectious. It was what Loretta imagined a happy ending was like. She finally found her peace. Her fairytale. Her Jim. But, just as all stories don't actually end, and all songs have layers to them, Loretta's life was no different.

After her set, she was expecting Jim as always. This time, he was late. Hours late. She sat with Joe as she wished he was just caught up somewhere. Usually Loretta would be on her way home by now, or out on her street-lit walks. *Where was he?* Loretta wondered. It was well past midnight and Jim hadn't shown up yet. She was starting to get worried. The words Jim said to her on the night they met rang in her ear like a song. *I have a funny feeling we'd make a perfect pair.*

The piercing sound of police whistles combined with a rough "Everybody out!" and bombarded the room. Jim was still nowhere to be seen. Loretta hid in the back-room door still holding onto hope that Jim might meet her later.

Joe confronted one of the three police officers, knowing that this was his goodbye to The Swanky Owl.

"Officer, fights happen here every night...it's the brandies."

The cop snarled and said, "We're not here for the fight, mister."

The lights came on. Loretta never saw the club this bright before, like it somehow snapped into the world above. She watched from a crack in the back-room door. The people in the club rushed out as if there was no tomorrow, like tonight was their last night to live. She saw an officer stand guard in front of Joe, keeping him with his hands behind his head against the bar. Accompanied by the itch to live were frantic breathing patterns along with a couple of squeals, mostly projected by women. The cigar smoke in the room disappeared as the club-goers did. So did the brandies. The club was washed out and pale like an old black shirt.

"Bring him in, Johnson," the third police officer yelled toward the alley door.

Loretta became a statue. Her feet were glued to the sticky floor as she saw Johnson bring her Jim inside, handcuffed. Johnson brutally shoved Jim into the first seat he saw. The last time she saw Jim with his hands behind his back was her birthday.

"Got him, Colby." Johnson snarled as he turned to leave the lifeless, washed-out room.

As she stared at her completely helpless Jim, she didn't feel herself leaning into the crack in the door. She fell forward, opening it, which left her completely exposed on the ground. Colby motioned to Johnson to start his trek toward Loretta. Jim's eyes met hers.

"Loretta," he whispered with a strain of shame as he slouched in the chair. Colby heard him. It took less than a second for an angry cop to glare unwelcome eyes into hers.

Confusion and fear took over Loretta's being. Her feet were magically lifted off of the ground by Johnson under Colby's orders. *So, this is what the club-goers felt like when Tiny came to break up fights.* Johnson put one hand on her shoulder, the other held her hands together behind her back. Colby turned back to address Jim.

"Does she work for you?" he said intimidatingly.

"No." Jim could barely get the word out.

"No?" Colby yelled into Jim's ear.

"No," Jim said with a loud cry.

Another police officer who was stationed outside came in with a message.

"They're ready for him."

Colby abruptly rose Jim to his feet. "All right, Jimbo. Let's go."

Jim could not lift his head to get one last glance at Loretta. Shame and regret were too powerful of sources to come out of. *Guilty* was marked across his forehead with permanent ink. Out the alley door, Jim went, beaten. The nameless cop who was standing guard of Joe let him go with a warning.

"We'll deal with you later," he said as he turned to leave.

Johnson let Loretta go with some advice, dropping his intimating nature just a tad.

"I would find another job if I were you."

He took a step closer to her.

"Besides, you're too good to be playing in this rotten place," he said as he smiled and turned to go.

Loretta felt broken. She wanted answers. With a spark, Loretta's timid curiosity turned into a flame of courage.

"Where are you taking him?" she said with as much firmness

she could muster to match Johnson's. He stopped and turned around to answer her.

"Ma'am, unless you have a god-awful lot of money, bail isn't gonna get him out."

"Just tell me, please. Where are you taking him?" Loretta desperately asked the officer.

Johnson stared into Loretta's eyes. He saw her heartbreak. He saw her confusion. He saw her longing for answers. Compassion from a police officer is mighty hard to find.

"Ma'am, you really do have no idea, do you?" he said as he took a step toward her.

All Loretta could do was shake her head as a response. She fought back the tears building up in her eye sockets.

"The 9th precinct," he said with as much comfort as he possibly could, and started toward the alley.

With those words, Loretta stood frozen for a couple of moments trying to catch her breath. She couldn't. So instead she ran toward the door, leaving Joe alone with his speakeasy and restaurant for the last time. When she got to the alley, she saw Johnson. They shared a quiet moment of unspoken under-standing.

He said," I can't promise anything," with a shimmered glaze in his eye that could only be formed by tears. After she watched the officers leave, Loretta's feet flew off into the night.

That was the last time she saw Jim. A week later, heartbroken, the club was closed down. Her whole world fell apart seven days ago. One night, as she helped Joe clean out The Swanky Owl, Johnson dropped by. He was not in his uniform. When he entered, he gracefully took off his hat and held it to his heart.

"Excuse me. Miss. Loretta?"

Joe and Loretta almost didn't recognize the kind-hearted man standing in front of them. Joe took a step in front of Loretta. He would never stop protecting her.

"It's alright, Joe," she said and he stepped aside to continue cleaning up the joint.

"Miss. Loretta, I've got some mighty bad news to tell you," Johnson said as he took a few steps forward to face her. This way she could see the sincerity in his eyes when he said his next words.

He took a deep breath and spoke the three words that would leave Loretta on the floor, devastated.

"Jim died last night."

Joe dropped the case of glasses he was holding, leaving a cutting mess on the floor. Loretta fell to the floor slowly as the grief worked its way through her body, diminishing all of the hope she ever had in her bones. Johnson took a knee and met her eyes. He reached out his hand to her shoulder to console her.

"Don't touch me!" she screamed as the hysterics from uncontrollable tears washed out her face.

After Johnson tried to offer his condolences, Loretta asked the only question on her mind.

"What happened?"

Johnson explained that he was stabbed in his cell by a police officer. After learning Colby was the button man, it was later discovered that Stan had put the hit out on Jim. After that, discovery changed its key once again, tying Stan to the Italian Mob, and the Italian mob had connections with the police. They had a hand in everything, and Stan was the right-hand man to the big boss. As it turned out, Jim wasn't a Real McCoy either. He was the newest recruit for the Irish Mob who have been on a jewelry store stealing spree and were connected to a slew of murder cases. The mobs were working together.

After Johnson explained all of this and the tides of emotions seemed to calm a bit, Loretta put some puzzle pieces together. The logic was not lost from her bones. The first night she met Jim and his sweatiness. The way Stan and Jim seemed to know each other. Her birthday present. She should have suspected. Somehow this all became her fault. She was Stan's girlfriend. She snuck around and fell in love with someone else. She did this. She was the reason he was murdered.

Not long after Johnson informed them he resigned from the police force and left the speakeasy, an older man around the same age as Joe came into the club.

"Hi. I'm looking for a Miss. Loretta Luna."

Joe suddenly had a spring in his step as he walked over to greet Mr. Cowl.

"Why, George! How are you?" Joe said as he shook Mr. Cowl's hand.

"Loretta, this is Mr. Cowl."

Loretta has never felt the whiplash from heartbreak, guilt, and loss, to happiness and hope before. She stood up from the chair she was sitting in, dried the wet streaks on her face, and walked over to greet the man.

"Mr. Cowl, it's a pleasure to meet you."

"The pleasure is all mine. I would like to speak with you about an opportunity," he said as they walked to an empty table.

Turns out, Mr. Cowl was the man to help her escape her trap of a life. Joe stuck by her side as her Fairy Godfather, granting all of her well overdue wishes. But every night on the Broadway stage or touring the world, she heard Jim when she played. Each note became his voice. She wanted to keep him alive, and this was the way she knew how. She kept him new. The Jim she remembered. Not the pale, old black shirt he became. Those ten words he said to her on the night they met never left her. *I have a funny feeling we'd make a perfect pair.*

Amanda Montoni is woman of many passions. She is a Director, Choreographer, Performer, Dance Teacher, Theater Teacher, music-lover, cat mom, and a co-founder of the Royal Star Theatre Company based in Queens, NY. Through her many years of being involved in the arts, writing has always been another constant in her life. Her intent is for readers to find solace and companionship in her work. Sometimes a hand just needs to be held.

https://www.amandamontoni.com/

5

GROWING UP IN THE SUMMER OF '71

DEBBIE DE LOUISE

I was Janey's little sister. The fattest girl in my fifth-grade class. I had no friends except my cats, my books, and my sister. Janey wore her long, honey-brown hair in braids tied with different colored ribbons. We both loved the Beatles, Carpenters, Carole King, Tony Orlando, and Dawn, and all the popular groups and singers of the '70s. She liked to dance to her 45's or the radio, and I would sing along to "Leaving on a Jet Plane," "Knock Three Times on the Ceiling," and "Maggie May."

It was the summer of 1971. I was 11. Janey was 21. Mama said she married my dad young and had Janey right away. I came along much later. I always wished I'd been closer in age to Janey.

Janey had a boyfriend named Johnny. He wore bell-bottom pants which meant the bottom of his pant legs were wide and shaped like bells. He also wore a beard, and I asked Janey if it tickled her when they kissed. She said it felt good. I caught her smoking behind the house. It didn't smell like daddy's tobacco, and she laughed a lot when I told her but still had me promise not to tell mama. She was glad Johnny wasn't leaving for Vietnam.

Mama called him a hippie, and Daddy didn't let him step into our house, but Janey said she loved him. She was moony over him.

In June, right after school let out for the summer, I got my first period. I thought I'd cut myself on the toilet. When I told mama, she apologized and said she thought I was too young to tell about lady's stuff. She sent me to see Janey who took me to the drugstore and bought me some pads. She told me she used tampons, but that I should be a little older to use those. She said I should be careful around boys now because I could get pregnant. I didn't have a boyfriend. No boy would like a fat girl like me.

In July, when Mama and Daddy had a big argument (I think it was about Janey and Johnny), but it might've been about how much money Mama was charging on her new credit card, Janey asked if I wanted to take a drive with her. She had her own car that she'd bought with the money she'd saved from her job at the diner. It was a used car, a 1965 Mustang. I loved riding with Janey. She was a good driver and didn't speed like our father. She'd taken lessons at a driving school because Mama didn't drive, and Daddy was too impatient to teach anyone anything.

Janey took me to Johnny's house. She told me Johnny had a younger brother who was 13, two years older than I was. Johnny was also two years older than Janey. She said that Robbie was actually Johnny's stepbrother. She explained that Johnny's dad was no longer married to his mom and that his mom had married again and had Robbie with her new husband. I didn't really understand or care how that worked.

I remember the long drive to Johnny's house. It seemed like it took forever, but I wasn't used to riding much except on the school bus. As soon as Janey parked in front of the brick house and we started up the walk, the door flung open and Johnny came out. Janey ran to him, and he lifted her up in the air and spun her around. He wasn't muscular, but he seemed to be strong.

When Johnny put Janey down, she was laughing and flinging back her braids.

"Hello, Lucy," Johnny said spotting me. "Why don't you come in? I'll get Robbie."

I entered the house behind Janey. It looked about the same size as ours. There were more knick-knacks on the shelves in the living room and many more photos. Our mama didn't collect anything, and she kept all our pictures in photo albums. I was fascinated by the tiny treasures Johnny's mom featured in a curio cabinet. I later learned they were from the many places she'd traveled with Johnny's dad riding a motorcycle. I saw her through the kitchen alcove, blonde hair in a ponytail as she stirred boiling water for spaghetti. She was plump but not fat like me. There was a trace of gray at her temples. She sang one of the popular tunes. Something about a stairway to heaven.

Before I could interrupt Mrs. Cotelli, Johnny stepped into the room with his brother. Unlike Johnny, whose blonde hair curled around his earlobes, Robbie had short dark hair with a trace of a mustache shading his upper lip compared to Johnny's full beard. He was slim and a few inches taller than I was and wore straight-legged slacks with a plaid shirt, but the thing I noticed most about him was his light blue eyes, almost the same shade as my Siamese cat's.

"Lucy, this is my brother, Robbie," Johnny introduced us. "Why don't you two sit on the couch and talk while Janey and I go outside? Mom will have dinner ready for us in a few minutes."

I knew that Johnny was going outside with Janey to smoke, and I felt uncomfortable being left alone with this boy who I didn't know at all. But Robbie smiled at me, and I liked his smile as much as his eyes and the way both seemed to welcome me, unlike the stares and expressions of the kids at my school.

"Nice to meet you, Lucy," Robbie said. "Your sister is very nice. She talks about you a lot."

"She does?" I didn't think Janey talked about me at all. Hearing that she did, made me happy. It was a feeling I wasn't used to.

"Yep. She told us you loved to read, and you also write stories."

Writing was something I was proud of but not something I shared with many people, not even Janey. I wondered if she'd somehow found my stories and read them, but I kept them hidden under my bed in the same notebooks with the black marble covers that I used for my schoolwork.

"Would I be able to read one of them?"

I don't know why, but looking into his blue eyes, I couldn't refuse. "Sure. I'll bring some next time."

His smile deepened, and I saw a dimple in his left cheek. I wondered if Johnny had dimples, too, but knew they wouldn't be visible under his beard.

Mrs. Cotelli called us to dinner. Johnny and Janey came back in, and I smelled the sweet smoke on Janey's gypsy skirt. It tickled my nose and almost made me sneeze.

Mrs. Cotelli had set the table in the dining room for five. I wondered if Janey had told her I was coming and why Mr. Cotelli wasn't there. She answered my questions when I walked into the dining room behind Robbie.

"Hello, there. You must be Lucy. Janey mentioned she might be bringing you to dinner. I'm so glad you could make it, and I see you've already met Robbie." She had the same light blue eyes as Robbie but little lines creased the sides of them. "Have a seat, honey. You and Robbie can sit together and Janey and Johnny over there." She pulled out our chairs and motioned to the ones across from us. "My husband is working late again, so it's just the five of us."

"Thank you, Mrs. Cotelli," I said.

"Please call me Angie. That's what my kids do."

There was a large, heaping bowl of spaghetti at the center of the table. Angie sat at the front and passed it around. When it came to me, I almost dropped it. I was afraid of embarrassing Janey, but she only had eyes for Johnny. She sat staring at him throughout the meal. Comparing the brothers, I thought Robbie was more handsome despite his youth.

After the spaghetti made its rounds, Angie passed a smaller bowl that contained the sauce and a serving spoon.

"This is delicious, Angie," Johnny said after he'd poured some sauce on his pasta and taken a few bites of spaghetti.

"My mother makes her own sauce from tomatoes she grows in our backyard," Robbie said, whispering to me. "After dinner, I can show you her garden."

"Angie, you must give me the recipe," Janey said, although I knew she'd never even boiled an egg in her life.

Angie's round cheeks turned red. "I use spices and fresh tomatoes in the sauce. I chop some onion and garlic and add them, too. One can never use enough garlic."

I wasn't a fan of garlic, but I hardly tasted it in the sauce.

"I couldn't believe it when Johnny told me he'd been to Woodstock," Janey said, changing the subject. I thought she was afraid Angie might actually give her a cooking lesson. "I wish I could've been there." Her eyes took on that dreamy quality that made me feel sick, like after I'd eaten too much chocolate from the candy store near the library.

Angie smiled. She also had a dimple like Robbie. "If Johnny's dad was still around, I'm sure we would've gone, too. That was one cool music festival."

I was surprised to hear a woman Angie's age use the word, "cool." Our mother never spoke like that. I looked around the dining room and noticed more knick-knacks lining the shelves and displayed in the china cabinet. Angie must've seen my interest because she said, "I loved traveling with John, Sr. I always picked up a souvenir wherever we went. We took lots of motorcycle tours, even one to the Grand Canyon." Her tone was wistful, and I wondered what had happened that they broke up. Janey said they were divorced. I couldn't understand why people could have so much fun together and even have a baby but then walk away from it all. Janey said I would understand when I was older. Mama and Daddy were still married, but they fought a lot. Maybe fighting wasn't such a bad thing. I imagined not talking at all would be worse.

When dinner was over, Janey helped Angie do the dishes. That was another surprise because she never helped Mama with chores. I was always the one to do that. She told me I should go outside with Robbie. I was looking forward to seeing the garden. We didn't have one at home because Mama said she didn't have a green thumb. I'd rather lay in a hammock on the patio and read or write. The people in my books and stories had such exciting adventures. The main character was usually a beautiful young woman who was in danger and was saved by a handsome man. Janey had been the one to get me started on what they called gothic romantic suspense novels. She'd given me a copy of Phyllis Whitney's *The Winter People* one Christmas, and I went to the library and checked out all the author's other books. Then I searched for authors who wrote like her and read those, too.

Robbie was proud of his mother's tomato garden. He said she also planted herbs to use in her cooking. He showed me around their backyard and then we sat on the patio swing talking until twilight set in at 8 p.m. He told me about his school and how he didn't have many friends. I couldn't understand that because he seemed very friendly.

When Janey came to take me home, she kissed Johnny, and we

looked away. Angie waved to us from the door as Janey started her car. Robbie stood outside waving to me. He'd asked me to come again and bring my stories the next time.

Janey had a best girlfriend. Her name was Molly, but she insisted everyone call her Starshine. Janey went to high school with her, and they continued their friendship after graduating. Starshine was a dancer. She worked in a nightclub, but Mama said it was a bar, and I was too young to go there. Janey met Johnny at Starshine's club. Starshine introduced them. That was last year, and Janey and Johnny have been inseparable since.

One day in late July, after I came home from school, I heard some weird music playing from Janey's bedroom that sounded like raindrops falling. Through the beads that covered the entranceway (Janey had Daddy take down the door and use a beaded curtain to separate off her room), I saw Janey and Starshine. Starshine was standing on her head. Janey was sitting cross-legged next to her the way they make us sit at school during assemblies. Starshine's long, blonde hair fanned out around her. She didn't wear it in braids like Janey but let it hang loose. It covered her back completely and even touched her tailbone. She wore a pair of faded jeans with peace and love symbols patched on them.

Both girls seemed to be in a trance of some sort. I had to call Janey a few times before she responded and, when she did, she was angry. "What are you doing here, Lucy? Starshine and I are meditating and practicing yoga. We don't want to be disturbed."

"Sorry," I said. "Is Mama home?"

"She went shopping. Get out of here."

Starshine rolled out of her yoga pose. "You don't have to be so nasty to your sis, Janey. She can stay if she wants. Maybe we can give her a lesson."

I didn't want to learn yoga. It looked silly.

Janey stood up and turned off her record player. "I have a better idea. Let's do our nails." She went to her bureau and took a bunch of colored polishes and nail polish remover from the drawer. I looked on in eager anticipation. There was nothing I enjoyed more than doing nails with my older sister. I wasn't allowed to put any polish on myself, but I had fun acting as a manicurist and painting her nails. She and Starshine were barefoot, their open-toed sandals pushed away in the corner. I saw that the old polish on Janey's feet was chipping and assumed her fingers would be worse. Starshine didn't have any polish on at all.

"I'll be glad to help," I offered.

Janey went to the bathroom and came back with a towel she spread on the floor. She and Starshine sat cross-legged on it. "Come on over," Janey told me. "You can do Starshine first."

Starshine smiled. I noticed how white and straight her teeth were. Janey's were stained from smoking, and she needed braces. So did I, but Daddy said we couldn't afford them.

"Why don't we put on music while we get our nails done?" Starshine suggested. "Take off the rain music and put on some JT."

Janey went to the record player. She flipped through some of the albums in the pile next to it and took a record out of one. As she touched the needle to the disc, the music for "Fire and Rain" began to play and then James Taylor's voice filled the room.

"Choose a color," Janey told Starshine. I was a little nervous because I'd only painted Janey's nails in the past.

Starshine rifled through the shades, finally picking up a rainbow-colored polish. "This looks groovy," she said. "I usually don't wear polish. Is this environmentally safe? Were any animals used to test it?"

"It's all-natural," Janey said. "I buy all my stuff at the natural cosmetics store. It costs a bit more, but it's worth it."

"That's a relief," Starshine said. "Okay. Paint me." She handed me the small bottle of rainbow color. I sat down next to her as she extended her hands.

"Wait, Lucy," Janey said, grabbing a clear polish from the ones on the towel. "Don't forget to use a primer first. The color will last longer."

I took the polish she handed me and began to paint Starshine's nails. I noticed they were cut pretty short, and they looked as if she bit a few. After applying the clear coat, I put the first coat of the rainbow polish on thinly as Janey had taught me.

"Now do mine," Janey said. "After you use the base coat, I want this color." She handed me a red that matched one of the colors in her gypsy skirt. Starshine was shaking her hands and blowing on her nails to dry them. I had to apply a second coat and also paint her toes, but I figured I'd start on Janey next.

When I'd painted both hands and toes of Janey and Starshine, Mama came home with the groceries, and I had to help her put them away. Starshine thanked me, and I think she liked how I painted her nails, even though she smudged the thumb afterward, and I colored one of her cuticles.

When I'd finished helping Mama, Janey and Starshine were gone. I found them outside smoking that sweet tobacco on the corner of the house when I went out to read my library book, *Mistress of Mellyn*, by a new author I'd discovered, Victoria Holt, who wrote the same type of gothics as Phyllis Whitney. When they saw me, they turned away. Janey knew I wouldn't tell Mama, but I think Starshine was embarrassed.

A week later, Janey told me Johnny was taking Robbie to the movies with her and asked if I would like to come along with them. They were going to see *Escape from the Planet of the Apes*. I remembered that I'd promised to bring some of my stories for

Robbie to read when I saw him again, so I told her I'd love to go and brought one of my notebooks containing a few of my recent stories.

"What do you have there?" Janey asked when I got in her car. "Are you bringing schoolwork to Robbie? I told you we're going to the movies."

I forgot that Janey didn't know about my stories, or at least pretended that she didn't. "Robbie wanted to read some stories I wrote," I explained. "A few of them are in this notebook."

"You can show him after the movie."

The movie was good, and Robbie shared some of his popcorn with me. I had my favorite Bonbons ice cream balls. He didn't seem to care or say anything about how much I was eating or that I was "fat enough" like some of the kids at school said during lunch periods when I ate alone.

I noticed that Johnny and Janey were watching each other more than the movie. They sat behind us. When I turned around once to observe them, they were kissing those deep disgusting kisses. I turned back to the screen.

When we were walking outside to Johnny's car (he'd driven us there after Janey had left hers at his house), Robbie whispered to me, "I think my brother is going to ask your sister to marry him." I looked at them holding hands in front of us. I wondered what Mama and Daddy would think of having a hippie as a son-in-law. "Wouldn't it be fun if we grew up and married, too?" I was surprised. I was beginning to think of Robbie as a friend, but I didn't expect him to like me more than that considering how overweight I was.

Back at the Cotelli's house, Angie greeted us in a flower-patterned apron. She was wearing the same type of sandals as Starshine had when I'd painted her toenails. I smelled the spaghetti sauce simmering in the pan as I walked in the door.

"Was the movie good, Kids?" she asked. Janey answered. "It was great." I knew she hadn't watched it at all so I hoped Angie wouldn't question her about the plot.

Since there was still time before the food was ready, Janey and Johnny went outside while Robbie invited me up to his room. It was neater than mine with a twin bed covered with a blue and white comforter that featured a space theme. Posters of rock singers filled his walls and there was one large poster of Apollo 11 with Neil Armstrong's quote, "One small step for man. One giant leap for Mankind." The U.S. spacecraft had landed on the moon just two years earlier in a historic television broadcast.

"You have a nice room," I told him.

"Thanks." He smiled. "Sit on my bed, and I'll read your stories."

I'd never sat on a boy's bed or even been in a boy's bedroom before, but I didn't feel uncomfortable. Robbie took my notebook and laid it open on the bed while he sat against his pillow. I sat by the foot of the bed. "I hope you like them. I've written others, but these are my latest."

"Give me a few minutes. You can check out some of my comics and toys while I read."

I walked over to the desk which had a world globe on it and a framed photo of Robbie, Johnny, and their parents. I noticed Mr. Cotelli looked a lot like Robbie with the same short brown hair and a fuller mustache. Besides the photos, a few hot wheel cars sat atop a stack of comic books and GI Joes stood patrol next to them. I carefully removed the cars and looked through the comics. There were some Batman, Spiderman, and Avengers, along with a couple of Archie comics. I took the Archie ones and sat back down at the end of Robbie's bed.

When I took a break from my Gothic novels, I'd walk to the drugstore and browse the revolving stand of comics. I'd save up the allowance Daddy gave me each week and buy about ten of them at a time. At 15 cents apiece, they were a great investment in entertainment. I was glad to see that I hadn't read any of the Archie comics that Robbie owned. While he was concentrating on my stories, I occupied myself with Archie, Jughead, Betty, and Veronica.

When Angie called up to us that dinner was ready, I reluctantly put the comics back on Robbie's desk. It was perfect timing for Robbie, who'd just finished the last page in my notebook. As he handed it back, I asked, "What did you think?" I was a little nervous because I'd never shown anyone but a few teachers my creative writing.

"I loved them," he said. "I really think they're good. You should be a writer, Lucy."

I wasn't prone to blushing like Janey was, but his words made me happy and slightly embarrassed. "One of my teachers said the same thing, but no one else has thought so." I didn't bother saying that I'd never shared them with anyone else because I didn't think anyone would care what a fat girl wrote.

"I'd definitely buy your stories if you sold them. Thank you for showing me, and please bring more next time you visit." I certainly hoped there would be a next time. I was becoming very fond of Robbie.

Janey was acting even moonier over Johnny than ever at dinner. Angie had to ask her three times to pass the spaghetti sauce before she heard her through her trance. I thought she was meditating again, but I found out what the problem really was when I drove home with her. In the car, she said she had a secret to tell me. It always frightened me to hear Janey's secrets because it wasn't that easy for me to keep them. I recalled the time that she played hooky from work at the diner to see Johnny perform with his rock band at The Digs, the club where Starshine worked. I don't know why she told me, but I ended up asking her how the concert went right in front of Mama. I would think she'd learn her lesson after that, but I guess she was so excited about the news she had to tell someone, and I was sitting in the car next to her for the half-hour drive.

"Don't tell Mama, but Johnny gave me a ring."

So Robbie was right. "You're getting married, Janey?"

She laughed, and it was a high-pitched giggle. "No, silly. If I were getting married, I would've screamed it all over the neighborhood. I'm not engaged yet, but almost. Johnny gave me a friendship ring. He hasn't told Angie yet, so I didn't want to wear it on my finger, but look . . ." She pulled the car over and took a chain out from under her sweater. A gold ring hung on the end of it.

"Is that real gold?"

"It might be. Johnny bought it with his money from the band. Next, it'll be a diamond. Lucy, this is the best day of my life. Just wait until Starshine hears."

For the next month, I was a frequent visitor at the Cotelli's home. Robbie and I often accompanied Johnny and Janey on their dates. We went fishing together, rowing boats out on the lake, to outdoor concerts, and bike riding in the park. I began to feel like my sister and her boyfriend's chaperone, but sometimes I felt like I was double dating with Robbie. We'd become very good friends over the summer. I'd shown him more of my stories, and we often took

walks around his neighborhood while Johnny and Janey were
spending private time together. On our walks, we talked about
books, movies, and kid stuff that I'd found hard to share with
anyone else. I began to wonder if what Robbie once said might be
true–that, when Johnny and Janey married, we would marry, one
day, too. I imagined what it would be like to be Robbie Cotelli's
wife and wrote the name Lucy Cotelli in my notebooks, the ones I
would never show Robbie.

It was at the end of August, a week or so before school would start,
that two significant things happened in my 11-year-old life. They
both happened on the same day. I was visiting with Robbie in his
house while Johnny and Janey were outside. We'd been playing
chess, a game Daddy had recently taught me. Robbie said he'd
learned chess from his father, too, and he seemed very good at it.
Rather than boasting about beating me, he taught me some moves
that would help me corner his king. When I told him that I
thought he was a good chess player, he said he wished he could be
as good as Bobby Fisher. I didn't even know who Bobby Fischer
was, but I assumed he must've played chess pretty well.

   After our chess match, Robbie asked if I wanted to play hide
and seek. He volunteered to be "it" first. I closed my eyes and
slowly counted to ten. I figured he would have the advantage
because he knew the best hiding places in his house. I hadn't
heard him go upstairs, so I figured he wasn't hiding in his
bedroom. I checked behind the living room couch first, but he
wasn't there. I looked in the kitchen under the table, but there was
no sign of him there either. I tiptoed down the hall trying to be
quiet, so he wouldn't hear me coming. I slipped into the first room
off the right that I figured was his parent's bedroom. I tried to
figure out where he would conceal himself in that room. I didn't

think he'd be under the bed, but I checked anyway. Not finding him, I surveyed the rest of the room. The lights were off, and I was afraid to turn them on. It wasn't yet night, so I could still see fairly well. I noticed one of the sliding doors of his parents' closet was slightly ajar. I hesitated because I feared Angie would walk in and think I was snooping, even though she was probably still out shopping. I approached the closet slowly. I could see a long dress hanging inside but not much else. I put my hand on the door and was about to slide it open further when Robbie jumped out. "You found me!" he exclaimed.

I jumped. He'd given me a scare. Seeing my reaction, he apologized. "Sorry, Lucy. I thought you knew I was there." He was looking at me in a strange way. In the shadowed room, I couldn't read his expression. Unexpectedly, he came close to me and brushed his lips against mine. I was shocked again, but I didn't move. The kiss was quick and nothing like the deep mushy ones Johnny gave Janey, but it was still a kiss. As we stood there, facing one another in the darkened room, a girl's voice called Robbie's name.

"Robbie, are you home?"

The moment was gone. "Excuse me, Lucy. I think that's Jill."

I followed Robbie into the hall where a girl about his age stood. She was wearing a pink tank top and cut-off jeans shorts. Her blonde hair was tied in a ponytail. But the main thing I noticed about her was that she was about 50 pounds thinner than me.

Robbie looked embarrassed. I wasn't sure if it was because this girl had joined us or if he was thinking about the kiss he'd given me. "Uh, hi, Jill. This is Lucy, Janey's sister."

He turned back to me. "Lucy, this is my neighbor, Jill."

In all the times I'd visited Robbie throughout the summer, I'd never seen Jill, but it seemed she knew Janey.

"Nice to meet you, Lucy." I noticed there were a few freckles spotting her cheeks. She was also tanned, as if she spent a lot of time at the beach.

"Hi, Jill," I said, trying not to stare at her spare frame.

"Robbie, I just dropped by to see if you wanted to go to the fireworks show at the park with me and my family tonight, but I didn't realize you had company." She looked at me through eyes almost the same shade of blue as Robbie's.

I felt uncomfortable. "I should be leaving with my sister soon," I said, although I had no idea how late Janey was planning to stay.

"I'll catch up with you later, Jill," Robbie told her. "Thanks for inviting me."

She smiled and then turned. "Okay. See ya later."

When Robbie turned back to me, he didn't say a word about continuing our hide and seek game or about what happened after I'd found him. I wanted to ask him about Jill and if they were good friends, but I couldn't bring myself to do it. I'd had my first kiss and my first taste of jealousy within a matter of minutes, and I was still trying to understand the emotions that both had stirred in me.

Luckily, Janey came in soon afterward and told me we were leaving. I wondered why Johnny wasn't with her. Her eyes looked slightly red as if she'd been crying, and I asked her what was wrong as she drove us home. Watching her hands on the steering wheel, I noticed that the friendship ring she'd recently started wearing on her ring finger was missing.

"It's none of your business, Lucy," she told me sharply. The rest of our ride was silent. She didn't even turn the radio on.

Even though Mama had meatloaf and her special mashed potatoes ready for dinner when we got home, Janey went straight to her room saying she wasn't hungry. Mama lifted an eyebrow, but I didn't think I should comment. I couldn't eat much either even though it was tasty. I slipped a few scraps of meatloaf down to Beatle, our Siamese cat, who always sat begging under the table when Mama cooked. After eating, I went to my room, too. I read a bit and tried to write another story, but my mind kept going back to Robbie, the kiss, and Jill. I was also thinking about Janey and what it meant that she wasn't wearing Johnny's friendship ring. Her room was next to mine, and I heard her crying into her pillow to try to muffle the sound. I wondered what would happen if Janey had broken up with Johnny. Would I be able to see Robbie again? The thought of not seeing him was painful. Thinking this, I also felt guilty because I was more worried about myself than Janey. I thought I should go to her and see what was wrong, but she'd closed herself off to my questions in the car.

As I lay there thinking about everything, another thought crossed my mind that really frightened me. I recalled Janey telling me after she explained about my monthlies that I should be careful around boys. Could I be pregnant? I wasn't sure if kissing made babies, and I figured that if that were the case, Janey would have had a dozen kids by now, but I heard her tell Mama once not to worry about that because she was wearing something called an IUD. I never noticed anything on her mouth, so I wondered where she was wearing it.

As Janey's sobs grew louder, I knew I had to do something. I got out of bed and stood by the beaded curtain. "Janey, are you okay?" I called to her.

The crying stopped and, in a few minutes, Janey said, "Come in, Lucy."

I walked through the beads pushing them aside with my right hand. Janey was sitting up in bed, a few tissues in her hand. I saw a large wet spot on her pillow. Her eyes were redder than they were in the car.

"What's wrong?" I asked. "Why are you crying?"

Janey sniffled. "I asked Johnny if he was thinking of proposing. It's been a while since he gave me the friendship ring. I just asked. I wasn't pushing." A few tears fell down her cheeks.

I went over to the bed and sat down next to her. "What did he say? Was he mad?"

Janey blew her nose and wiped her eyes. "He said he wasn't ready to commit. He said he was seeing someone else."

"No one could be better than you," I said, trying to make her feel better. "He'll come back."

"No." She choked back a sob. "It's Starshine he's seeing. They've been dating all along, and he never told me. She never told me. It's over, Lucy. Mama and Daddy were right that he's just a hippie and has no future. I have to find someone else."

"What about Robbie?" I asked, almost regretting the question because it would make me seem selfish.

"I'm sorry, Lucy, but I won't be going there anymore. You'll have to find another friend."

Didn't she realize that no one else would want to be friends with a fat girl who spent her time off from school daydreaming about stories and reading books about beautiful women she'd never grow into?

I started to cry. I didn't want to, but I couldn't help it. I knew it would only make Janey feel worse. I thought about Jill and how lucky she was to be Robbie's neighbor. I lived too far from him and wasn't old enough to drive, so it was likely we would never see one another again.

"Men can be so cruel," Janey said. Her eyes were clear now, and her voice sounded angry. "You're better off without any of them." Was she talking to me or to herself?

"But what if I'm pregnant?" I asked. I don't know how that slipped out, but Janey's eyes grew wide. "What are you talking about, Lucy? You didn't sleep with Robbie, did you?"

"Sleep with him. No. We were just playing hide and seek, and he kissed me."

She looked relieved. "Is that all? He just kissed you?"

"Yes, but I wasn't wearing an IUD."

Janey's laughter filled the room. I was glad she was no longer crying, but I was puzzled about what she found so funny about my answer.

"Lucy, I thought Mama told you about the birds and bees. I guess she left that up to me."

"I've read lots of books about birds and bees."

Janey smiled. "That's not what I meant. Before we go into all that, I want you to know that you're a beautiful, sweet, and smart girl. Don't let anyone make you feel less because of your weight or anything else. I've always been proud to have you as a sister. Knowing about boys involves more than how babies are made. It involves feelings and emotions, and maybe those are the hardest lessons we need to learn." She opened her arms, and I leaned forward for a hug. I was sad about losing Robbie, as I knew she was sad about breaking up with Johnny, but her words made me feel better about myself.

I guess Janey's little sister was growing up.

Debbie De Louise is an award-winning author and a reference librarian at a public library on Long Island. She is a member of Sisters-in-Crime, International Thriller Writers, the Long Island Authors Group, and the Cat Writers' Association. Her novels include the five books and three stories of the Cobble Cove cozy mystery series, a comedy novella, When Jack Trumps Ace, a paranormal romance, Cloudy Rainbow, and the standalone mysteries; Reason to Die, Sea Scope, and Memory Makers. Her latest book, Pet Posts: The Cat Chats is a non-fiction pet book. She lives on Long Island with her husband, daughter, and three cats.

Debbie's stories and poetry also appear in the Red Penguin Collection anthologies, What Lies Beyond, 'Tis the Season, Stand Out: The Best of the Red Penguin Collection, Volume 1, and A Heart Full of Love. Her poems are also featured in the Nassau County Voices In Verse 2020 anthology and the 2020 Bards Annual.

https://debbiedelouise.com

6

HOLLOW GLITZ

OLIVIA ARIETI

Natalie married Franco for his money and the convertible blue Cadillac he ostentatiously drove down the High Street. Both were aware of that, but neither minded. A sumptuous house, expensive clothes and lots of fun were what the girl had always been after and no one better than the shady gangster could satisfy her whims and wishes. The guy, on the other hand, was unable to love, a sort of immunity that helped him succeed in his promiscuous affairs. He wasn't estranged to beauty, though, and that's why he fell for the loveliest flapper in town and married her. The union, however, didn't imply letting down the less gorgeous ones he used to visit; morals were a nuisance that would never keep him away from lust's bed.

Unscrupulous and conceited, the couple walked the path of glamour where everything was allowed as long as it was dazzling, entertaining and outrageous.

Those were the days when nights gleamed with pleasure, and cocktails, jazz and the most extravagant parties animated all hearts and seemed to dispatch forever loneliness, boredom and guilt.

The doubt that Franco could have killed her brother, Joe, often crossed Natalie's mind, but, too busy in her personal affairs of vanities and fearful that the truth might threaten her wellbeing, she refrained from investigating.

The suspicion never faded though and always flashed before her when they made love. Her husband was a true boss in bed, too, but the following day new gowns and lingerie often accompanied by a precious collier or ring were the rewards for her assent. That, too, was part of the deal.

Being a gangster's wife made Natalie look intriguing and desirable; forgetful of the nights in the squalid saloons, whereby flapping her arms and sending out bewitching glances she enticed her vicious guests, she swayed from one party to the next, glittering in gold and kindling men's desires and ladies' envy.

As time went by, all glamour seemed to vanish; parties were called off, the flashy gowns became worn rags and cheap booze definitely deposed champagne.

Franco grew tense as the fright of the impending financial disaster began to afflict whoever was in business, whether legal or not. Misery and decay were at the door. The more depressed, the more he frequented his old girlfriends. Their company made him feel good, their caresses even better. Worries didn't intact his seductive charm and each of the pretty slags was sure his pockets were still full of dirty bucks.

Gossips, however, spread quickly and Natalie's friends now made fun of her.

"So it's hard to keep the ladies' cake all for yourself?" or, "Have you stopped flapping for him?" were the questions always followed by derisory giggles.

Anger and solitude replaced merriment and despair rose when she spotted the first wrinkles on her face. The lack of money also caused the loss of resplendence as beauty salons and makeup were too expensive.

When her old fiancé, Lewis, came back to town with a wallet bursting with bills and as handsome as a movie star, the flapper poured out all her grief and asked forgiveness for walking out on him, unaware that the gentleman's love had turned into deep resentment.

The bloke had never recovered from the fact that his best friend had stolen his bride-to-be and spent the past years excogitating how to take revenge on both cheaters.

His timing was perfect; he would accept the girl's favours and, once in possession of her heart, now apparently quite vulnerable, he set his requests.

One evening, sure of her feelings, he whispered while unzipping her dress, "Two men are too many for you, baby, you must get rid of one."

"You know I want *you*, sweetheart," she replied languidly.

"That's what I hoped to hear," he said and let his lips run down her back.

"There's only one way out, kill Franco and you'll be totally mine."

Natalie turned around and gazed at him. His glance was mandatory—no smoother way of eliminating his rival, now also a strong competitor in the newcomer's criminal business.

The killing was unexpected, shocking; running away with her lover would have been less complicated–no gore, threats or farewells, and the fun would start again.

Lewis didn't know that his generosity lured her more than his affection.

"Aren't you being too hard on him, dear?"

"Not as he's been on me. He's taken away my most precious

thing" and added, "I was too poor to fight the bastard those days, but now I can afford it."

For a second, Natalie felt flattered. Could vanity turn her into a murderer?

The thought diverted her and made her smile assentingly, as if making a half promise.

"I won't wait long," the fellow warned during their last encounter. "Patience is for losers, doll."

Then he handed her a gun with a silencer, "The quickest and most discreet way to solve the matter."

An ongoing anxiety seized Natalie; Lewis's demand was a true menace to her glitzy existence that was about to take off anew.

While lost in a maze of doubts, her husband entered with a bunch of roses.

"I'm a lucky guy, sugar, just bumped into the biggest opportunity of my life," he said and took out a diamond bracelet. "It's been quite long since I gave you a present, but from now on you'll have whatever you wish once again."

Then he served her a glass of champagne.

"I want you to forgive me, sweetie, you didn't deserve all that slush."

The tiny bubbles sparkled as ever and their delicate bitterness together with Franco's gift and words showed their effect.

"Put on something fancy, and we'll go straight to the governor's party where all the most respected ladies in town are dying to meet you."

Natalie was taken aback. *Respect* was a discarded word and *authorities* a most dreaded category. Surely, with his delinquent manoeuvres he had managed to reach the high spheres and subdue the rest of the crooked gang to his will and power.

She had just finished her drink and was about to leave the room when he stopped her.

"Wait, dear, I want you to know the truth about Joe."

Since when did he care about the truth?

After a moment of silence, he continued, "I wasn't aware of the trap... The murder was carried out behind my back, believe me."

She smiled feebly, more amazed by his attitude than relieved by the revelation.

Somehow he appeared changed; his manners were unusually gentle, the double-breasted jacket very becoming, and the grizzled hair, even if too slick and shiny, made him look less vain.

The revolver was still in her bag. She could have taken it out and fired at him, but did she really want to? The twinkling of the diamonds reminded her that money had started to roll in. Why go through unpleasant situations when there was no need to? Besides, her feelings for Lewis were already fading. What looked like the awaking of a genuine emotion was nothing but sloppy sentimentalism due to frustration. The guy wasn't worth it, she said to herself as she powdered her cheeks.

Franco's image appeared in the mirror; his hands on her shoulders made her shiver. "There's something else, baby," he sneered. "Your old boyfriend, Lewis, was the bloody creep that killed him. You had to know it sooner or later."

Natalie glared at him, horrified. His expression and the tone of his voice was definitely provocative... For sure, he was aware of her affair, but never would let his rival have her.

Was he also aware of the gun in her bag?

She wondered if he would kill him or if he was tacitly inviting her to do it...

Then he took her in his arms and kissed her passionately, so as to leave her breathless. That was his way of asserting his claim on her.

Perhaps he hadn't changed at all, but, as usual, she didn't care. Joe was dead and nothing could bring him back. True, killing Lewis would have served him good, perhaps with that same gun he gave her, but why should she get in trouble for him? He wasn't worth that.

She took out her most gaudy dress and snickered; nothing better than shining before those hypocrite ladies and watching them melt with jealousy. Her rags had suddenly turned gold and her eyes gleamed with sensual wantonness. Franco would be hers from then on and everybody would acknowledge that.

Even if the couple didn't love each other, they still enjoyed staying together—the deal kept working and Natalie felt comfortable and light-hearted once again. Also, Franco was satisfied; he had the most gorgeous and devoted wife in town and, even if with more discretion, he carried on with his encounters, not to mention that Lewis was found dead shortly afterwards.

After all, their relationship was the perfect embodiment of the spirit of the age and neither their minds nor hearts could be aware of its limits.

Olivia Arieti was born in Pisa, Italy, spent her childhood in Miami Beach, her teen years in Detroit, Milan and now lives in Torre del Lago Puccini with her family. Besides writing and reading, she loves walking her four dogs. She writes drama, poetry and fiction.

7

ANOTHER MOUTH

TERRI PAUL

COLUMBUS, OHIO: JUNE 1930

I take a sip of my inky-brown coffee. It's as bitter as the gaunt man who looks up at me from the front page of the Columbus Citizen. "40,000 Ohioans Out of Work," says the caption beneath his photograph.

Someone pounds on the kitchen door, probably Jimmy Janowitz from across the alley coming to beg for food. Mr. Janowitz, one of the 40,000, vanished in January, leaving Jimmy and his mother nearly penniless. How I wish I had more to offer than an end piece of challah, all that remains of last night's dinner, and a brown banana my younger sister Kati forgot to eat yesterday.

"Jimmy," I say as I fling open the door.

"I am no Jimmy!" Papa growls and tries to push past me.

Blocking his path, I step onto the back porch and give him a hard stare. We're eye-to-eye since I'm eighteen and only half an inch shorter than he is. I haven't seen him in almost a month, and he's much the worse for wear. His collar is threadbare, his pants filthy. Black stubble bristles from his chin. His ten-year-old step-daughter Lorrie squeezes his hand. Her skin is gray, and I wonder how long it's been since she had a decent meal.

"Sarah," he says. "I must talk to your mother."

"She is at the store," I say. "You know that."

"Damn!"

"Papa Sol!" Lorrie says. "Ma told you not to curse."

He winces at the mention of her mother, his second wife who died of pneumonia this winter. He often drops Lorrie at our house like a load of laundry on Saturdays and hurries off, likely to sell his bootleg whiskey. On the Sabbath, no less. He always says his customers can't be kept waiting. Today is Thursday, so something's up.

"I'm on my way to the store," I say. "I will tell her you were here. You could come back later."

His voice rises. "I cannot do that. It is a matter of life and death. Take the child. Go and find her."

"I want to stay here with you, Papa Sol," Lorrie says.

The clench of his jaw softens. He looks almost sad. "Next time."

I slam the door behind me. Mama doesn't trust Papa alone in the house. His fingers stick to coins on the kitchen table or our silver saltshaker, a gift from the rabbi's wife that disappeared after he showed up.

"Hey, Lorrie," I say. "I bet you a nickel Mama will give you a treat,"

"A chocolate peanut butter cup?" she asks.

I coax her down the steps. At the gate, she turns to wave at Papa. He's leaning against the wall, his chin buried in his chest. He doesn't wave back.

The grocery store, which Mama bought with her divorce money, is three blocks to the east. Mr. Geller, the previous owner, came to Columbus from Berlin before the Great War and returned home two years ago because his daughter, my best friend Annalisa, was unhappy here. I'm worried about her, considering Mr. Hitler and everything that's going on in Germany.

"Papa Sol has no job," Lorrie says. "There is no food."

"What about your grandfather and their furniture business?" I ask. "I thought the two of them were buying and selling and making loads of money."

Mr. Abrams, Lorrie's grandfather, is the one who put the idea of selling used furniture into Papa's head in the first place—and the one who supplied him with all the money he lost after he divorced Mama and married Mrs. Greene.

"All gone," Lorrie says. "Papa Sol told me Grandpa doesn't love me anymore."

"That is not true," I say.

"It is so. Grandpa ran off with our money."

You mean his money, I think.

"That's why Papa Sol has to find him," Lorrie says. "If you won't...if I can't stay with you, I'll have to go to the Jewish orphanage on Parsons Avenue."

"That terrible place," I say. "Mama will never let that happen."

Lorrie hiccups. "After Papa Sol sold Ma's piano yesterday, my cat Morton ran away. I went searching for him. It was dark when I got home. Papa Sol was mad. He thought I'd hopped a train."

"How? You are just a little girl."

"That's what he said. That's why he has to give me away."

"He's not giving you away."

She squints into the sun. I wipe away a tear on her cheek.

"I never had a brother or sister," she says. "Father died when I was a baby. Will you be my big sister?"

I hook my arm through hers. "Of course I will."

The store is just ahead, and we stop to look at the words

"Geller's Kosher Market" painted in bold black letters on the window.

"Who is Geller?" Lorrie asks.

"The man who used to own it," I reply.

"Did he die?"

"No, but his wife did. The last I heard he was in Switzerland with his second wife."

Lorrie frowns, clearly thinking of her own mother. "Second wife..."

The grocery doesn't open for another fifteen minutes. We find Mama at her desk in the storeroom, hunched over a ledger. Once the stock market crashed last September, money grew tight. She doesn't have the heart to refuse families like the Browns, who have four shoeless children, and we spend more than we earn. Can we afford another mouth to feed? Maybe, if the Schillers and the Solomons settle their accounts with us today.

"Papa is at home," I say.

Mama purses her lips.

"He needs to talk to you," I say. "I can stay here with Lorrie and mind the store."

"I want Papa Sol," Lorrie wails. "Sarah, you have to come with me."

5 June, 1930
  75 Stralauer Street
  Berlin, Germany

Hello dear Sarah,
  I have bad news. Grandmother dies four weeks ago. She has

seventy-eight years. I tuck her in bed. Weather is warm. She does not wake up next morning. I telephone doctor. Hooligan stops him in street. Tries to rob. Says he is "rich Jew." Something else he does not repeat. He comes to us. Grandmother is gone many hours. I wish I am in room with her when she dies. I am asleep then.

Father travels from Switzerland for fortnight. He brings wife Liesl. She cleans. Shops for food. Makes big dinners. I am not hungry. I am crying. She talks. I am silent. She is not happy. I hurt her feelings. Father's, too. I am sorry.

They return to Switzerland. Wish I come too. Liesl has three children, all grown. They are from first marriage to dead husband. Also, Father fears Hitler's hatred for Jews. One week ago, friend and I enter restaurant. Two police at door ask how old. We say eighteen. Ask are we Jewish. She says yes. So what? They tell us to leave. I try to push by. They tear my blouse. Call me something filthy. Grab my purse. Shove me. I fall and hurt knee. I have black scab.

Father telephones me. I tell story. He says I must come to him. I do not want to live as stranger. In new country with no one to talk to. Except Father. I do not want Liesl for mother. Mother and Grandmother are dead. No one takes that place.

Mr. Berger, Grandmother's lawyer, says I must sell furniture. But I must give away part of Mother and Grandmother every time someone buys. Mr. Berger urges to remove Grandmother's savings from bank. And go. Most German people have no money. Or money they have is worth nothing. They say Jews steal. Mr. Berger believes things get worse.

House is different. He must file papers for deed to me from Grandmother. Then I sell or government takes. Mother is child here. So am I. Rooms remind me of long-ago. But past is gone forever.

I continue art studies at academy. We finish fruit and flowers. I think people are more simple. I am wrong. We draw hands. I cannot fit

all fingers and thumb. Palm is too small. Fingers are too long. I feel fool-
ish. Professor says only Leonardo paints hands correctly.

I practice English one hour each day. Can you tell? You remember I
was in Columbus. We write essays about books at South High School.
You try to improve me. I am rude. I do not want to learn. I wish to be
with boys.

I apologize. You are kind to me.

Yours with love,

Annalisa

Back home, the stoop is empty, except for two lonely pillowcases full of Lorrie's belongings piled next to the door. Papa is gone. No surprise. He's good at disappearing when things go bad.

Lorrie's lower lip trembles. "Papa Sol."

"Kati is upstairs," I say, referring to my younger sister who's a bookworm. She and Lorrie share a love of reading. "Let's go up to the attic to see her."

"But I want to wait for Papa Sol."

"Let Mama do that."

I hustle her into the house and up the stairs. I knock on Kati's door.

"It's me, Sarah," I say, letting us in. "You have a visitor."

Kati is sitting in bed, propped up against the wall. She glances up from the book in her lap, her eyes wide. "Lorrie, what are—"

I press a finger over my lips. "Lorrie really wants to see you."

"Can we read more of Little Women?" Lorrie asks. "Can we?"

She rushes across to Kati and plops down next to her. Kati sets aside the book she's reading and grabs a volume with a dark green cloth cover from the pile on her nightstand. Lorrie takes her peanut butter cup out of her skirt pocket and unwraps it halfway.

She bites into it and smiles. Her top teeth are covered with choco-late. Kati opens the book and begins to read out loud. I slip into the hall and go back to the kitchen. Lorrie's pillowcases are lying on the table.

"How long will she be with us?" I ask Mama. "Forever?"

"We will never live to see the day," she says.

"She can have Sam's old room. He's so busy at the university he's hardly ever home anymore."

"What a good idea."

"I'll help Lorrie put her things away and be back in the store in a half an hour."

"I can manage without you until then. Perhaps I'll leave early and prepare a special dinner. I can telephone Sam and ask him to come."

"Lorrie adores him. That might take her mind off her troubles."

I lug Lorrie's things to Sam's room and find a set of fresh sheets in the hall closet. I call up to her, and she comes skipping down the stairs. Her cheeks are flushed, as she babbles about the book, Papa forgotten for the moment. Sam has the best room in the house. It's in the front of the house and has two windows and a soft bed on the far wall.

"How do you like it?" I ask.

"Fine," Lorrie replies. "But where will Sam sleep?"

"He only comes home when he wants a decent meal. Besides, this is the biggest of all of our bedrooms You are lucky."

"Lucky..." she murmurs, not sounding convinced.

We shake the contents of her pillowcases onto the bed. I wonder where her lacy blouses and patent leather shoes have gone. Did Papa leave them behind? Or worse yet, sell them? I wouldn't put it past him. Her blue eyes are moist, and tears stick to her long lashes.

"I want to go home," she says.

"I know," I say. "But being here is not so terrible. You have Kati to read with and me to talk to. We will have fun this summer. You'll see."

She stares at her fingers. Her nails are blackish pink where she has bitten them to the quick.

The day passes quickly, and by the time I get home, Sam is hovering over a large pot of stuffed green peppers that simmers on the stove. Kati and Lorrie troop into the kitchen.

"Who's been sleeping in my bed?" Sam asks.

"I...I can find somewhere else," Lorrie whispers.

"Don't tease her, Sam," I say.

"Why not? Come here, Goldilocks."

He grabs her and tickles her under her chin. She giggles and pinches his arm.

"Ouch," he cries.

"Serves you right," I say.

After Kati and Lorrie set out our dishes and silverware, we gather around the table and dig into Mama's peppers.

"I feel like I ate a watermelon," I say, once the pot is empty.

"Many people are not so fortunate," Sam says.

"We must always appreciate what we have," Mama says.

"Herbert Hoover is a do-nothing," I say. "We need a new president."

"I agree," Sam says and pulls a cigarette from his shirt pocket.

"Can I have one?" Kati asks.

"You are only a child," Mama says.

"Hardly. I'm fifteen. Older than Sam was when he started."

Sam inhales deeply, blows a smoke ring that lingers in the air above us, and rolls his eyes.

Sunday, June 15, 1930
 693 East Mound Street
 Columbus, Ohio

Dear Annalisa,

 Did you realize your grandmother was sick? You never said so. It is painful when someone you love dies. I told you about my Uncle Josef. One minute he and I were talking happily in the front seat of the truck. The next minute Papa skidded on the ice and crashed into a tree. My uncle was gone. That was four years ago. It does not hurt as much now, and I can laugh at the funny things he said. That would make him happy. I am sure your grandmother would want you to remember her with a smile. She would not want you to be sad.

 We read about Mr. Hitler in the papers. His hatred is a disease. Mama thinks you should move to Switzerland. Sam, Kati, and I do not agree. We think you should live your own life. Or you could return to the United States. You could stay with your cousin Bettina in New York City. There are many universities that teach art. You could earn your degree AND be an ocean away from Mr. Hitler. Or you could come to Columbus. Mina graduated from Pharmacy school last spring and moved to Cleveland, so there is an empty bed in my room. The art school here in town is a few blocks away from the grocery. I can find out more about it, if you want me to. It would be great fun to have you here, and I will do everything I can to help.

 Yes, your English is improving. Not a single German word anywhere. Did you use a dictionary? Do you speak English with the other students at the academy?

 Our customers still ask about your father. Miss Newman from Feinberg's Finery across the street always wants to know whether we have gotten a letter. The tailor at the end of the block and the pawnbroker across the street—their doors are padlocked. Some of their windows are

broken, which breaks my heart. It is fortunate for us no one can live
without food.

It is getting late, so I will stop writing.
With love from your friend,
Sarah

~

Footsteps on my bedroom floor wake me from a half-sleep, and Lorrie whispers my name. I roll onto my side. Her face is pale in the moonlight, and her hair falls into her eyes

"Why aren't you asleep in your own bed?" I ask.

"There were spiders on Sam's window. Long, skinny ones with tentacles."

She shivers and slides in next to me. My room is hot, so I touch her forehead to check for a fever. Her skin is cool and dry. I fluff up the feathers of one of my extra pillows and place it under Lorrie's head. She settles into the crook of my arm.

"It must be at least midnight," I say with a yawn.

"Whenever I couldn't sleep, Mother would tell me a bedtime story," Lorrie says. "Will you tell me one?"

"About what?"

"Papa Sol. How did he bring your family to Ohio from Hungry?"

"Do you mean Hungary? It could take forever."

"I'm not tired."

"I am."

"Tell me, and I promise I'll go to sleep."

I begin with the morning Papa disappeared from our village when I was four because he owed everybody money and couldn't pay his debts. Lorrie's body tenses for a moment. I draw her closer and she relaxes a bit.

"Go on," she says.

"Mama told everyone she didn't know where he was," I say. "I used to imagine him sliding off the roof of our shed or riding on my teacher's shoulder. When he didn't come back, Mina and I were sure he was dead. So we hatched a plan."

"What kind of plan?"

"We snuck away to a funeral at a synagogue in the next town."

She gulps. "I hate funerals."

"So do I. Anyhow, we sat in the back of the sanctuary where no one would notice us and prayed that Papa's soul would fly into the dead man's casket. It didn't work. I looked up, and Papa was perched on the elbow of a woman in front of me. He winked at me."

Lorrie laughs out loud.

"Shh," I say. "Kati is next door, and the walls are thin."

"What happened after that?" Lorrie whispers.

"The Great War started. We had to leave our village and go north. It was my first train ride. I was six."

I don't add that the Hungarian army stopped the train and took our engineer and locomotive. Or that it was ten days before someone rescued us, and we almost starved to death.

"Have you ever been on a train?" I ask.

"Once when Mother and I went to Cincinnati to see her cousin," she replies and starts to cry.

"Afterwards, Mama and the four of us children lived in a shack for two years. And guess what?"

She wipes away the tears shimmying down her cheeks. "What?"

"The one school for miles around was a convent. We had to attend Friday Mass. Mina loved Catholics, especially the nuns."

"I don't like nuns. Their robes make them look like bats."

She shivers again, so I skip over what it was like to return to our village. How it belonged to the Romanians; how everything of ours was gone, including the brass candlesticks we used on the Sabbath; how ragged we were after we left our village and walked for two days to our grandparents' house. We stayed with them for a while. Like Lorrie, we had a family, but we weren't home.

"Don't stop," Lorrie says. "Tell me the rest."

"Will you go to sleep?" I ask.

Yawning, she stretches her arms over her head. "I promise."

"Many months passed. A letter arrived."

"From Papa Sol?" she asks.

"He invited us to come to Columbus."

"I might get a letter like that from him."

"You might." I hope she doesn't hear the lie in my voice. "We took a train to France and boarded a ship to America. Here's the very best part. Sam turned thirteen and had his Bar Mitzvah in the middle of the ocean."

"He did not!"

"It was in a big room in the bottom of the boat. There was a minyan, and I watched from behind a bale of straw."

She sighs."

"We sailed into the harbor," I say. "The Statue of Liberty was so beautiful I wanted to climb into her arms. Papa was waiting for us."

"Papa Sol..."

"I saw Houdini hanging from a tall building and ate my first ice cream cone. We were home at last. In America."

"America..."

"We took the train to Columbus and lived happily ever after."

"Happy..."

Lorrie begins to snore. I brush her hair off her cheek. Her journey with Papa has hardly begun, and I wonder if it will have a better ending than mine did. I cover her gently with my sheet and nestle close to her. The steady sound of her breath puts me to sleep.

Terri Paul is a novelist and poet. Her book GLASS HEARTS (Academy Chicago, 1999, 2013) won the Friends of American Writers Award and the Ohioana Book Award in fiction. Like "Another Mouth," it is based upon the recollections of her maternal aunt, who long ago told Terri about how the family came to America from Hungary. Terri is currently working on two follow-up books to GLASS HEARTS. "Another Mouth" is excerpted from the first chapter of the third book. Please visit https://terri-paul.com for more details about her writing.

8

GIRLS JUST WANT TO HAVE FUN

ELAINE DONADIO

"Ladies, this drink is not for the faint of heart. It's guaranteed to get your buzz on," our server warned us. "Remember, sip."

"Well, Franco, that sounds exactly like what we need." Miss Ellen turned to me and with a girlish giggle belying her years, toasted to my health, "À votre santé, dear Patrice."

"And to your health, too, Miss Ellen."

We clinked glasses of Long Island Iced Tea, gingerly sipping our tall drinks.

Living vicariously through the escapades of the rich is what my life has become. Being employed as a sidekick to a wealthy *grande dame* of Southampton, now well into her nineties, certainly has its perks. I answered an ad some years ago advertising a position immediately available for a *simpatico* woman for a very special lady. Being some twenty-five years her junior, I'm spirited enough to keep up with Miss Ellen, but happy to know there are limits to her energy.

Miss Ellen chose this venue for brunch knowing this multitiered restaurant/club is the hottest place for young people in Hampton Bays. Piped in music played in the background while the band set up. Cyndi Lauper. Michael Sembello. Billy Joel. Journey. The most popular performers of the day provided an energetic backdrop. Plenty of young people having a good time.

There we were, protected from the beating sun by a bright orange Sunbrella, ensconced in our eagle's nest enjoying the last hurrah on the saddest day of summer—Labor Day—with an enviable panorama of the bay and more importantly, an unobstructed view of the action surrounding us. A great place to people watch. Things have certainly changed from when I was a girl.

In my younger days, my mother often gave me advice about how a lady conducts herself in order to convince an eligible bachelor to give up the single life to become a husband, successful breadwinner, and father. In those days it was not common for young women to pursue higher education, so my mother was adamant against my desire to follow my dream of becoming a teacher and continuing to work if and when I were to marry. "If and when you marry? You cannot be serious. No self-respecting young woman would ever say such a thing. Patrice, a man does not want a wife who is smarter than he is. What you're proposing is... scandalous! I will not allow you to entertain such thoughts."

"But, Mother—" I tried to reason with her.

"There are no buts about this. Where are you getting these revolutionary ideas? Oh, yes, it was those Suffragettes who planted seeds of these unseemly thoughts, protesting and making demands. Because women have the right to vote now, you think we are equal to men? No, we are not. Where did it all lead? To the flapper era—that's where—with women defying society. Drinking alcohol. Cursing. Smoking cigarettes. Driving automobiles. Flaunting their bodies. Sexually free without the benefit of marriage ..."

"But, Mother," I tried to reason with her. "Look at what they all accomplished for the women's cause."

"If women married, stayed home, and raised their families as God intended, they wouldn't need any causes."

"Sorry, Mother, but your ideas are antiquated. This is 1931. When you were a young woman Theodore Roosevelt was president. He rode a horse to battle, for heaven's sake. Things have changed. You should be happy about the great strides women have made."

"No, I am *not* happy. You will keep your legs and your bosoms covered at all times—not like those flapper girls. You're already seventeen. Your full-time job should be finding a suitable husband."

"Do you expect me to stay in this house, hiding from the world, hoping some perfect man will walk through the door with an engagement ring?"

"Hmmm. Good point. If you must work, you may take a job at the public library. They're looking for someone to check out books at the front desk. And, that is where young men of good breeding and worth can be found—not at a speakeasy."

"Mother, do you seriously believe I will find my Prince Charming at the public library?"

"Listen to me. I am smarter than you think."

On a brighter note, listening to my mother got me married to a wonderful man. Where do you think we met? The public library, of all places! He was studying to become a doctor, taking advantage of the quiet library to ponder his textbooks. We would whisper when no one was looking, and before you knew it, he waited for me to get off work so he could walk me home. We were married after he completed his residency. We had a long, happy marriage. Together, we raised two wonderful sons, who married and moved with their families all the way to the west coast for new job opportunities in computers/electronics in Silicon Valley, California.

My husband chose to practice on the North Fork of Long Island where we were both born and raised. He was a small-town doctor with a modest income who still managed to accumulate some money. Not knowledgeable about investing in the stock market, he did it the old-fashioned way—in a savings account at the local bank, collecting interest, not dividends!

We had a simple lifestyle but there was little money left in our bank account after we paid for our sons' college educations. After my husband passed away, my spousal Social Security benefits only went so far, so I had to find ways to supplement my income. And, so... here I am.

Nothing was then as it is now. The landscape was covered with potato and duck farms, migrant workers, and fishermen's shacks. The Long Island Expressway, completed about eleven years ago in 1972, changed all of that as it slowly inched its way east, taking more than three decades to span Queens County to – Eureka! – County Road III Exit 72. It amazes me that this once uneventful terrain is becoming a playground for the young, the beautiful, and the wealthy. Looking for fun? The Hamptons is the place.

"Patrice, are you not feeling well? You're a million miles away."

"I'm so sorry, Miss Ellen. I was remembering how things were so different for young women when I grew up."

"Imagine how *I* must feel. I was born in 1888," she laughed. "This is quite a culture shock. But... I've been taking it all in. Loving every minute. Here I am, reduced to being a voyeur—spying on the unsuspecting." Miss Ellen took another sip of her drink. "I've been watching those girls at that table," she whispered. "There seem to be new rules which make no sense to me. Young men try to talk to one of them, but the other girls vehemently repel them."

Sweet Miss Ellen. Widowed for many years. Born and raised in Charleston, South Carolina, an unwilling transplant, as a consequence of marriage, to the tony incorporated village of Southampton, south of Route 27, of course, on Long Island's South Fork, outliving her adoring husband and her beloved children. Grandchildren off to the four corners of the earth. How does a woman who devoted her life to her family find herself alone, paying for companionship, relying on the antics of strangers to fill her day with meaningful memories? Actually, we are not so different. I cannot pay for companionship but am eternally grateful for the opportunity to spend my days with Miss Ellen. Giving me a sense of belonging and purpose, I treasure the roles we play in each other's lives—loyal friend, trusted confidante, and constant companion.

My attention was abruptly diverted from my musings by a ruckus at the nearby table.

"Hey, baby, you've got one bitchin' bodacious bod," a young man raised his bottle of Coors beer. Tall, broad-shouldered, wearing light-colored blue jeans and a neon green T-shirt, he was at the height of fashion.

"Word," the young woman answered, giving him the once-over, then a dismissive snarl. Turning to her girlfriends, she rolled her eyes and pursed her lips, "It's my new Opium perfume. He can't help himself. It drives them wild."

"Get lost, loser," the young woman's redheaded friend yelled.

"You think you're too high class for me, or somethin'? Let me start over. Pardon me, would you have any Grey Poupon?"

"Gag me with a spoon," said her friend with the side ponytail.

"Are you always in such a heinous mood? You need a chill pill."

"Is this your brain on drugs?" asked the frizzy-haired friend.

I suppose the neon green T-shirt had enough insults. He walked over to his friends who were standing at the bar, laughing at the interchange that just occurred. "I told you she was trouble," one of the young men chided. He pointed to the image of Harrison Ford in Raiders of the Lost Ark on his T-shirt, "It would take someone like Indiana Jones cracking his whip to get that one in line."

"When did women get tougher than men, that's what I want to know?" the neon green T-shirt asked.

"Oh, come on now, don't let it get to you," Bon Jovi T-shirt said. "Look at her. All decked out like Madonna. Mini-skirt, off-the-shoulder-top, black lace fingerless gloves, stiletto high heels. White lace scarf tied in a bow on the top of her head. She needs someone with movie star looks."

"And you think that's you? You're the pretty one here, why don't you try and see what happens?"

"OK. You're on." Bon Jovi T-shirt walked over to the Madonna impersonator, trying to act nonchalant. "Do you have a light?" Bon Jovi T-shirt asked while pulling out his pack of Marlboros.

"Nobody smokes anymore. Do you think you're cool with your Air Jordans? Puleeeze. Get lost, Dork!" yelled the redheaded girlfriend.

With his eyes downcast, the young man quickly walked away. "So much for my charm and personality."

Neon green T-shirt patted his rejected and dejected friend on the back, "Let's get out of here."

With that, Raiders of the Lost Ark T-shirt spoke up, "Why don't we walk down to the beach for a while? I could use a change of scenery."

"Oh, you're leaving? Is it something we said?" asked the side ponytail girlfriend.

"We're out of your league, dudes," said frizzy-haired girlfriend

As the young men walked away, the very surprised Madonna look-alike called out, "Why are you dudes leaving? Afraid of a little challenge? I can't believe you're giving up so easily."

Needless to say, the young men did not turn around.

Miss Ellen turned to me in amazement. "Can you imagine anyone finding a husband, or even a boyfriend, with that attitude? I am shocked. Things have certainly changed from when I was a young woman, but not for the better."

Miss Ellen brings her genteel ways to a modern world that often finds good manners to be outdated and unnecessary, but I had to agree that I've never witnessed such deliberate disrespect, especially in a social setting such as this. I didn't want to be rude, but I found myself staring at the girls, open-mouthed.

The Madonna look-alike immediately noticed the expressions on our faces. "Ladies, do you believe those idiots left? I can't believe they just walked away."

"My dear girl," Miss Ellen said, "Are you saying you are surprised at their reaction?"

"Yes, I am. Totally. I got all dressed up to come here today. Everyone said I look so good. So why did they leave?"

"Do you not recognize your part in this?"

"What part?"

"Well, you might look pretty, but your friends were rude and insulting while you flaunted yourself, and you didn't say one word to stop the aggression. And you wonder ...?"

"I was playing hard to get. I like that guy with the green T-shirt. I've seen him around a few times. He's really nice. He shouldn't have given up. Well, he hates me now. I lost my chance."

"My dear, you need new friends. Those girls did everything they could to make sure you didn't get any male attention. They know you're much more attractive than they are and set up barriers to keep serious attention away from you."

"I never thought of it that way. You're right. This happens whenever we go out together. I guess I blew this chance today."

"Well, maybe not," I said. "I can't claim to be an expert in the charm department, but Miss Ellen was quite the belle of the ball in her time. I believe she was known as the foremost flirt in Charleston. Isn't that right, Miss Ellen?"

"Yes, thank you for remembering that, Patrice." Miss Ellen turned back to the Madonna look-alike, "If you're interested, I'd be happy to teach you all that I know."

"Really? That's so cool. I'm Nicole, by the way."

We introduced ourselves. Nicole called out to her friends, "Girls, I'm going to be busy for a while. Catch up with you later."

"What's that supposed to mean?" the side ponytail friend asked.

"It means not now. I'm busy."

I excused myself to go to the restroom while Miss Ellen and Nicole were deep in conversation. Looking over the rail, I spotted the neon green T-shirt and his friends standing at the shoreline, talking quietly. They seemed to be a congenial group—much nicer than those horrible girls.

My thoughts went to my grandchildren living in California. They are about the same ages as the young people here. That's how I know these recording artists. Trying to keep up so I can be thought of as the *cool* grandmother and not just another old person out of touch with the modern world. All these young people, single and ready to mingle, as they say. I wondered if my grandkids encountered the same situations in their dating lives as what I saw today. More like a war of the sexes than a mutually beneficial social gathering. Looking for love in all the wrong places, as the song goes.

The sound of guitars, drums, and keyboard filled the air as the band began their much-awaited performance. Young people congregated, leaving the beach and lower level behind. As if Mr. Neon Green T-shirt had a personal invitation, he and his friends staked their spots in front of the band.

Ms. Ellen and Nicole were busy writing on cocktail napkins. I couldn't imagine what Ms. Ellen had in mind, but she had a cat-that-ate-the-mouse expression while Nicole grinned from ear-to-ear.

Ms. Ellen beckoned me over to our table.

"Wish me luck," Nicole said.

"I do wish you luck," I answered. "What's the plan?"

"I don't want to jinx it. You'll see."

"I have complete faith in you," Miss Ellen encouraged Nicole.

After Nicole left, I tried to question Miss Ellen about what was about to happen, but she wouldn't have it. "Wait and see," she said. "Keep your eyes on our two major players."

A few minutes into the music, I saw Nicole ask the young man next to her to pass a cocktail napkin to the neon green T-shirt. He looked puzzled when he read what was on it and turned his head to see who had sent it.

"That note says: '*Hi, handsome!*'" said Miss Ellen.

A few minutes later, another cocktail napkin message was passed over. This time, he showed the note to one of his friends who shrugged. They both turned around but couldn't see anyone who looked responsible.

"That note says: '*I lost my phone number. Can I have yours?*'"

A short while later, the band's lead singer announced that he had a message for the handsome man in the neon green T-shirt. Then he read it aloud.

Roses are red.
Violets are blue.
My friends can be jerks,
This is true.
If you're willing to give me a chance,
I'd like you to know I'm ready for romance.

There was only one man wearing a neon green T-shirt. Yes, Mr. You-Know-Who. The audience clapped and whistled. "Hey, man, who's that from?" asked Mr. Bon Jovi T-shirt.

"I'm not sure."

With that, another cocktail napkin note was delivered: *I lost my white lace scarf. I think you have it. Can you bring it over to me, please?*" When the neon green T-shirt turned around he saw the white lace scarf hanging on his shoulder. "How did this get here?" When he turned to look over his other shoulder, he saw Nicole waving at him, smiling.

"I guess this belongs to you," he said as he got closer.

"Hi. I'm Nicole. Nice to finally meet you."

"Yeah, well... I'm Dave and I'm more than a little confused. What's going on?"

"I'm sorry for how my friends acted before. I didn't get a chance to say anything but I didn't want you to leave."

"You didn't?"

"You walked away before I could stop you."

"Really?"

"Can we start over?"

"Yeah, we can do that. We can definitely do that."

"Thank you."

"Did you make up those messages and the poem by yourself? That was so cool."

"No. I had help from a very special friend."

"Wow. This whole thing is unreal. Let's go sit on the beach— away from your friends and all these prying eyes. I feel like the whole place is staring at us."

"That's because they are."

They turned around to see all eyes on them. Nicole's girl-friends were ripping mad—arms crossed, scowling faces—while Dave's friends were smiling. Everyone else seemed happy as the scene unfolded. Miss Ellen's flirting tricks worked. Would anyone believe where they came from?

You're probably wondering how I could recount this entire conversation. Well, by prearrangement, we had a front-row seat since Nicole stood next to our table when Dave brought the scarf to her.

Months have passed and they're still dating. Nicole says if they become engaged and married, we're invited to both parties.

Miss Ellen and I can hardly wait. What fun!

Author. Poet. Blogger. Book reviewer. Reading Specialist at New York City Schools, Elaine Donadio's characters reflect the urban lifestyle. She writes about what she loves, using well-researched facts to feed your head, your heart, and your soul. She's concerned about the effects of human carelessness on the world in which we live. Learning is the point but better viewed through experiences that communicate awe as the world unfolds its secrets. Readers can laugh and learn at the same time.

Study guides in alignment with state standards for science, social studies, and literacy are available at elainedonadio.com.

9

THE SOCIAL EXPERIMENT

ANITA HAAS

"We have to tell him, guys." Chris blurted, interrupting their snorts of laughter.

Mark and Curtis looked at him, open-mouthed and frowning.

Curtis was the first to speak. "What do you mean, man? The fun's just starting!"

"Well, I just think that we should cut the thing short. It's gotten a bit out of hand. This could ruin his life. I say we tell him, or we stop it."

"*Shhhh!*" Mark silenced him. "Here he comes!" and raising his voice, he turned to Curtis "So, what did you think of the game last night?"

Chris rolled his eyes. How *obvious!* Mark had no subtlety. But then again, it was Russell they were duping, and Russell had proven himself to be the easiest dupe of all.

"Hey dude!" Mark turned to Russell, feigning surprise. "I didn't see you there!"

The three of them shifted a little to make room for Russell at their usual table in the corner. He put his tray down, completing the quartet.

"Hi," Russell said, pulling the chair out, and sitting down. He didn't look at any of them, he was smiling so much. He had been like this for the last three months. Ever since the experiment began.

"How's Trish?" Mark asked him a little too loudly, a little too interested.

"Oh, she's just fine." Russell grinned, blushing slightly and looking down at his untouched plate. He took a sip from his water glass, nearly spilling it, his hands were shaking so much. He was visibly bursting at the seams with his news.

"Only fine? Nothing new?" Curtis persisted. Chris shot him a warning look.

These guys were such insensitive jerks. How could he have gotten involved in this scam with them? And to think that it had been his, Chris's, idea. His only consolation was that poor, naïve Russell would never suspect. Not in a million years.

It had all started three months ago, right here at this same table in the lunchroom. Russell had been off sick for a few days with his asthma problems, and the topic of conversation had logically turned to the absent member of the group.

"Hey, what if we found our little buddy a girlfriend?" Mark began.

Chris smirked and Curtis snorted into his Coke glass. "Come on, man! Where are we going to find him a girlfriend? The guy stutters, he smells bad, he lives with his mom, and he can't even look you in the eye when he talks. He's gotta be a virgin!"

Mark insisted "I dunno. There's got to be somebody like him out there. Some poor, shy, ugly girl looking for love."

"Get real! Any girl would take one look at him and run."

"But what if she didn't see him?" Chris added.

The other men turned to him, perplexed, and Mark asked "What do you mean, man? Find him a blind girl?" Then they both broke out into their characteristic snorts.

"No. I've heard of people meeting on the internet. You know, chats, Facebook, that sort of thing ..."

Mark looked at Chris like he was a bit stupid. "Sure, but you need the other person to be there, be interested. I mean, we can't just *invent* the girl, can we!"

And that was how Trisha Shandy came to be.

Chris provided *Trisha* because that was the name of his first love, and Curtis thought up *Shandy*. He thought it sounded sexy. Too sexy, Chris thought. He probably got the name from one of his porn magazines. It was a bit suspicious. But then, stretching the limits was part of the game. How far could they go without giving themselves away? Chris was sure that it wouldn't go far, even if their guinea pig was known as the company idiot.

But the experiment had worked too well. Since Chris was the only one of the three who could spell, he had been delegated as the writer. They opened a Facebook account, found a sexy photo of a busty, good-natured-looking blonde, named her, and gave her a home in a faraway city.

Then the fun began.

At first, the posts were innocent, mundane, and Chris was sure they would all grow tired of it soon enough. But then one day, Trisha received a private message from Russell that practically broke Chris's heart.

Dear Trisha, You have no idea how alone I feel in this awful world. I know I am the joke of both my family and my colleagues. They all laugh at me. I have no idea how to change that situation. Maybe it is just my Fate. But when you came along ... You have been so kind to me. You are the light in my darkness.

These insights into his unhappy colleague's mind made Chris feel more tenderly towards him. He showed his cohorts, but they were not moved the way he was.

"This is amazing, dude!" Mark laughed. "Can you believe the poor dope thinks a real girl would actually pay attention to him?"

"Yes, but I think we should really stop it here." began Chris. "She could tell him she is getting back with her ex, or some story like that."

"What do you mean? Just when things are getting a bit interesting. And think about it this way, this is the first time I've seen Russell so happy."

Chris had to agree with that. Since the game started, Russell had become increasingly sociable. He even asked about their wives and families. He had remembered Curtis's birthday. His work was improving as well.

"Well, I don't feel too good about it, but maybe just a bit longer. Just to see ..." Chris's voice trailed off. See what? He decided not to think about it.

Chris continued writing to Russell in the voice of Trisha. He found that Trisha was changing him, too. He came to love Russell as one does a half-wit younger brother who gets bullied in the playground, while Mark and Curtis taunted him more than ever. When Russell confided his troubles to Trisha, Chris would console him through her.

The problem was that, since Mark and Curtis also knew the password to the page, Chris could not hide things from them. He could only discourage them from reading the messages, or delete them in a hurry before they got a chance to see them.

"What's new with our little lab rat today?" One of them would ask at lunch when Russell had gone off to the bathroom.

"Nothing special. You know." Chris answered, hoping they would get bored with the game. And, after a few weeks, they did. Chris thought that would be the perfect time to put a stop to it, but somehow he couldn't. Trisha had become part of him. She had literally given him a new outlook on life, seen through the eyes of a good-hearted, sexy, busty, but a little over-the-hill blonde. And part of the view was his defenseless, little buddy Russell. He couldn't leave him now, he thought protectively. What would the poor little guy do out there in the world on his own without Trisha to console him?

But then *this* had to happen.

Chris had been called away to an important meeting. It went on a lot longer than he had expected. Curtis, on the other hand, found himself with practically nothing to do that morning. So, he decided to check in on Trisha.

"Oh my God, dude! You have to see this!" he called to Mark in the next cubicle.

Mark strolled over and peered at Curtis's computer screen, "Holy shit! And he's already bought the ring and everything!"

Curtis was shaking as he tried to control his laughter, "And submitted his letter of resignation, and bought his plane ticket!" Tears were streaming down his face.

Chris stepped out of the boardroom. He wanted to get to Trisha's account before those other clowns did. Things had been heating up recently, and he suspected something big was going to happen soon.

But as he walked across the office floor, he saw them both huddled in Curtis's cubicle. He knew he had arrived too late.

And here they were at lunch, just an hour after the discovery.

Mark insisted. "You sure there, buddy? Nothing new at all? I'd have thought that by this time you'd be asking her to ..."

Chris was just close enough to kick Mark under the table.

"Well, a ... actually ...", Russell prepared himself to share his big news.

Mark and Curtis perked up. "Yeah? Yeah? Go on ..."

Chris's stomach lurched. He pushed his chair back, got up, and ran to the bathroom. It felt like he was throwing up everything he had eaten in his life.

When there was nothing more to eject, he went over to the sink and rinsed out his mouth. He splashed water on his face and examined his reflection in the mirror. He got ready to face them.

"Hey everybody!" Mark, the loudmouth was standing on his chair trying to get the attention of the other colleagues in the lunch room, while Russell sat red-faced and grinning stupidly, Curtis's arm around his shoulder. "This calls for a toast ..."

"Get down, Mark," Chris ordered.

Mark turned around, surprised, "But ..."

"I said, *get down!*"

Luckily, Mark had not attracted too much attention yet, and the few people who had turned around merely shrugged their shoulders and turned back to their lunches.

The three of them looked up at Chris expectantly. Chris stood at one end of the table, next to Russell. He bent towards them slightly, took a deep breath, and began quietly, "Russell, Trisha doesn't exist."

Both Mark and Curtis began protesting.

"Come on man! You are so damn boring!" Mark accused him.

"Yeah, Chris! How can you say that to our good buddy here?"

"Yeah, dude! Just when we were celebrating his..." Mark broke into exaggerated hysterics and couldn't finish his sentence.

Russell watched them, his face growing white. Chris saw something like a flash of understanding in the poor man's eyes.

He stood up slowly and with more dignity than Chris could have imagined. "I see." was all he said before turning around and hurrying out of the room.

Chris watched him helplessly from the table.

Russell drifted to his cubicle. It was a good thing he hadn't actually submitted his letter of resignation yet. He still had the receipt for the ring. And his mother had made sure his flight could be refunded if necessary. Somewhere deep down, neither of them had truly believed it could be real.

He sat down heavily in front of his computer. He had a lot of work to catch up on, that was true. But always, before starting work at the beginning of the day, and after lunch, he checked in with Trisha. He hesitated, then began typing.

Twenty minutes later, Chris stepped onto the office floor. The two loud mouths were already working seriously at their computers, having forgotten all about their lunch time entertainment. He glanced over at Russell's cubicle. He saw him working away as well. As if nothing had happened. He debated about passing by and saying something. But what? Something like *Hey, sorry about that, dude. No hard feelings, I hope? Buy you a beer after work?*

He sat down at his computer instead. He had a lot of work to catch up on, that was true. But always, before starting work at the beginning of the day, and after lunch, he checked in with Trisha.

There was one new message.

Are you there Trisha? They just told me you don't exist. I under-stand. That is very sad for me. But I was wondering. Could we keep writing anyway? Please say yes. Your faithful Russell.

Chris went cold. He sat motionless for several moments, then started typing.

Yes, Russell. I'm here...

Anita Haas is a differently-abled Canadian writer and teacher based in Madrid, Spain. She has published books on film, two novelettes, a short story collection, and articles, poems and fiction in both English and Spanish.

Some publications her fiction has appeared in include Falling Star Magazine, The Tulane Review, Literary Brushstrokes, The Zodiac Review, River Poets Journal, Scarlet Leaf Review, Terror House Magazine, Wink and Adelaide Magazine. She spends her free time watching films, and enjoying tapas and flamenco with her writer husband and two cats.

10

POCKET WATCH

ROBERT A. MORRIS

Enzo scraped the dried blood from his cuticles with his thumbnail. Entering the sanctuary, he noticed the same stale sweetness from years before. It was floral but heavy, a cross-pollination of candles and incense. He listened as the sopranos lifted the melody above the rafters and the tenors counterpointed below. Closing his eyes, he imagined the notes fitting together like pieces of stained glass. He translated the Latin, "Now dismiss your servant in peace..." Words came slowly for him, but music formed effortlessly from his breath. He thought back to when he also wore a red robe and congregated with other "song birds." That was what the older boys called them. They would rip his robe and tear out tufts of his hair. Once he cut it short and oiled it slick against his scalp to make this difficult, but they held him down anyway and cut his face with a sharp rock. The scar had almost healed, but he could still feel it as he ran his fingertips across his face. Looking around, he saw a nun directing the young singers. She was tall for a woman which made her eye level to the crown of his head. She summoned the flow of music with her long, elegant hands. Enzo recognized her. It was Sister Martina. She had aged but not badly, the veneer of youth receded to reveal a more substantial beauty. As a boy, Enzo secretly dreamed of her touch, if only hand to hand. He imagined the color of her hair under the coif and veil, the softness of it, the smell of it, maybe even seeing a loose strand curling against the nape of her neck. His cheeks felt hot as he thought back. He estimated her age to be ten years older. That would put her in her early forties. But maybe, it was less, closer to his own. Looking down, he turned towards the door.

"Enzo?" She asked, walking towards him.

Enzo hid his dirty hands in the pocket of his coat as he turned around. He paused awkwardly and asked, "You're still here?"

"I left and came back." She twisted the corner of her mouth and continued. "My papa passed away. I went back to Malta to be with mama, but she sent me back to America to continue God's work. How about you?"

"I am busy with my work too."

"Surely, you still sing?"

"No." The word came out louder than he intended, a lump the size of a pocket watch in his throat. "I lost my voice."

"You never lose your voice. Sometimes, it changes, but you will always have your gift."

"No one's ever given me a gift."

"Everyone has a gift, and yours is your voice." She smiled."The only thing you lacked is confidence."

"Well, I got plenty confidence now, traded my singing for it." His words came out raspy as he softened them.

"You can't barter for confidence. You have to develop it. You were smaller than the other boys. That is what made it difficult." She bent her head down so that she was looking him in the eye.

"I wasn't much smaller." Enzo straightened his back. A stray hair fell in his face.

"Do you remember that Christmas, I let you sing 'Ave Maria' and you were scared?" She turned around and drew a line in the air with her index finger. The singers stopped and exited, their red robes flapping like wings as they went out the side of the sanctuary.

"I wasn't scared." The hair tickled his nose.

"Do you remember how I told you I felt afraid when I left Malta to come here? But I found an object to focus on instead of my fear. I showed it to you and let you hold it while you sang." She stepped closer. "That was the last time I saw it."

"I gave it back." Enzo smoothed the hair back in place.

"I never told you but that watch was a gift from my papa. He was a fisherman, and it was the only nice thing he owned. He gave it to me the day I left home for the convent. It had an engraving of coast in Malta."

"Why didn't you tell me that?"

"I expected you to do the right thing."

"Maybe, I lost the watch." Enzo looked at his scuffed brown shoes. "The bigger boys would rag me about being a singer. They used to push me down and take my money. Maybe they stole the watch?"

"So you don't have it?" Her hands balled into fists.

"Let me make it right." Enzo reached into his coat and took out a roll of cash. His bruised hands struggled with the gold clasp.

"You're hurt." Sister Martina touched his palm and ran her fingertips across his sore knuckles. "Are they broken?"

"Bones heal." Enzo squeezed her hand.

"But they must be put in place to heal straight." Sis. Martina tried to slide her hand loose.

"You're right." Enzo held it tight.

"Your money doesn't help. I want the watch because it was papa's."

Enzo released his grip, but she let her hand rest for another moment.

"So, you will sing? 'Ave Maria' just like when you were a boy."

"My singing voice is gone," Enzo said, "but I have other talents. One day, I will be rich and I'll make everything square."

"God doesn't want your money."

"At least, I'm offering something."

"You can't just offer God what you want to him to have."

"So what does he want?"

"He wants all of you, and he will accept nothing less."

"Wish you wouldn't have put it that way, sister." Enzo looked at the windows. They were decorated with a mosaic depiction of Peter and Andrew abandoning their nets to follow Christ.

"I will give you time to do what you came for." Sister Martina said, sliding her hand away from his. She walked towards the choir loft and clapped for the singers to resume their positions. They resumed their positions, a flock of cardinals nesting in a tree.

Enzo watched as she motioned for them to begin. They were all attractive kids, tall and smooth-skinned, no runts. The voices wove together as he walked down the aisle. Stopping at the altar, Enzo peeled off three hundred from the stack and dropped them in the collection plate. He buried his hands in his pockets as he pushed the door open with his shoulder.

After rolling a cigarette, he popped the watch open with his thumb, a half karat diamond indicated the twelve o'clock position, rectangular emeralds marked the hours, and the outside was engraved with the sun over the open sea. Five o'clock and almost dark, he thought, I still got two collections left then a load of booze to deliver.

He snapped the watch shut and slid it in his pocket next to a flask and a set of brass knuckles. He turned around for one last look, his shoulders slumping under a secret burden.

Humming to himself, he rephrased the choir's hymn, its melody broken and sweet as birdsong, the words indiscernible except for "release, servant, and peace."

Robert A. Morris lives near Baton Rouge. He has recently completed a collection of poems titled Descending to Blue. The story "Pocket Watch" started off as a character sketch for a longer work set in Prohibition-era Chicago. When not writing, he bangs out the occasional song on his blue Stratocaster. His work has appeared in Lummox, Main Street Rag, Oyster River Pages, and other publications.

https://robertamorrisblog.wordpress.com

11

TIME IS HERE AND GONE

WILLIAM JOHN ROSTRON

"It keeps on getting better,
How life keeps movin' on.
Children growing older,
Seems I just looked over,
Found that time was here and gone."

\- Doobie Brothers

(1900 – 1970)

(1900 to 1910)

"Lost Little Girl"

"Think that you know what to do?
Impossible? Yes, but it's true."

- The Doors

He was a citizen of Rome. He had prayed in St. Peter's, stood under the Sistine Chapel, and seen the pope more than once. He had walked under the Pantheon's dome, toured the Coliseum, and thrown coins in the Trevi Fountain. He loved Rome and had done it all. However, that was the past. His future lay in America. He had a cousin who had gone there and had written back of all the opportunities. He was going. The new century would find him in the New World, but not before a farewell visit to a little farm village about seventy miles outside the city.

Posta Febrino did not have much. The poor farming village only had electricity in the richest of homes. The few roads *not* made of dirt were those left behind by the Roman Empire two thousand years before. The houses were clean but small, and the farms just larger than oversized backyards. But the village did have one thing that drew the ambitious Domenico Cippitelli to its streets...Lucia Longo. Though Lucia was young, barely sixteen, the city boy had seen her while visiting some of his country relatives and immediately been infatuated with her beauty. After a few chaperoned dates, they decided to marry after he found his fortune in America. By then, Lucia would be almost twenty, an old maid in the eyes of her peers.

However, this is what Lucia wanted. It would be a chance to see the world, and it would be a chance to be with the man she thought she loved on an exciting adventure. Whenever a letter arrived from New York, Lucia would sit excitedly with her eleven-year sister Filomena and read it to her. It was difficult. Both Lucia and Filomena had only four years of education before being forced to quit in order to spend their time watching their six younger siblings while their parents tended to the family farm.

As the years passed by, Lucia grew fearful. Since she had difficulty reading Italian, what would she do in a country where everyone was reading, writing, and speaking a language unknown to her. Were the streets really paved with gold, as she had been told? Why had Domenico not sent for her after five years? She confided her fears only to Filomena, who lived vicariously through her older sister. She hardly could remember the face of her suitor and as she stood on the threshold of spinsterhood in the eyes of her village.

Who really was this Domenico? How could he ask her to wait so long for marriage? How could he ask her to forego her youth and perhaps happiness waiting for him? In the end, she gave in to her fears. Once available, the suitors were numerous, and she soon found herself engaged to a fine young man who came from a good family and had inherited a farm twice the size of the Longo land.

. . .

The very next week after her engagement was announced, the letter came. Domenico now had an excellent job in a lumber company, and he had purchased not one home but two and rented the second out to relatives. He was doing well and wanted Lucia to join him. He sent the money for a boat ticket and told her that he would be waiting patiently to see her.

Lucia's answer described her plight and begged his forgiveness. She explained her fears of spinsterhood and her fear of an unknown country and language. Domenico never wrote to Lucia again. His only contact with the Longo family was a two-word telegram he sent to Lucia's father.

The entire village looked in wonderment as a Western Union messenger rode his bike through town. Because this was such a rare occurrence, a crowd formed at the Longo homestead as the stranger knocked. When Emilio Longo answered, the messenger handed him the short message. Shocked, he opened it at his front door as his entire family, and most of the town watched. Without thinking, he read its contents out loud, *"Send Filomena."*

With the Italian equivalent of five dollars in her pocket, Filomena Longo left Posta Febrino, Italy, at the age of 16. With only a canvass bag filled with clothing and some food, she made her way to the port city of Naples. Overcoming her fear and loneliness, Filomena set out on the long voyage to America. She had read every one of Domenico's passionate letters to her sister and felt that she knew the man she was to marry. Perhaps, she even loved him.

· · ·

She was joyfully met by Domenico at the docks in Manhattan on a warm summer day in June of 1901. For reasons of propriety, she was temporarily housed with female Cippitelli relatives. In September, they wed. Domenico and Filomena were happily married for half a century and had seven children.

And Lucia? She married and never regretted her decision not to leave her village. She never saw her sister again because of the distance between their homes. However, there were no hard feelings. Domenico and Filomena named their first daughter after the person for whom they had both felt deeply. That child, my grandmother, *Lucia* Cippitelli, was born in 1905.

(1910 – 1920)

"Immigrant Song"

"How soft your fields so green,
Can whisper tales of gore,
Of how we calmed the tides of war."

- Led Zeppelin

The Industrial Revolution was winding down in England. The once-booming textile mills were decaying. They were being replaced by brand new facilities in the United States, which had the advantage of home-grown cotton, thus sparing them the extra cost of importation that the English endured. However, there was hope for those workers in England who were skilled—these brand-new mills of *New* England were recruiting them.

And so, it was that John and Mary Ellen, and their three teenage sons set off for America in 1911. However, they were not just moving toward something new but also running away from tragedy. There had once been seven sons. Over the span of a decade, four of them had died tragically from different diseases and at ages from infancy to adulthood. Who remained were John Jr. (19), Harry (14), and (Fred 12). The sons, for their part, were not happy. Torn from almost everyone and everything they knew, they clung to their family—immediate and extended. Three of their father's brothers had preceded them to America. With their cousins, the boys could at least play football. The Americans didn't know the game, and the few who did called it soccer for some reason.

Their first year was a time of adjustment to the eccentricities of their new country. They had moved to New Bedford, a small city in the southernmost reaches of Massachusetts. Once the world's whaling capital, it had lost this industry to the nation's decided preference for oil drilled from the ground rather than harvested from a whale. Facing economic ruin, New Bedford shifted to textile manufacturing by luring the overflow of business from nearby Lowell's manufacturing center. In 1914, everything changed for this immigrant family.

· · ·

On June 28, 1914, Archduke Franz Ferdinand of Austria-Hungary was assassinated, and this lit the fuse for a war that would involve 60 million Europeans. However, the United States of America did not enter the war, at least not immediately. While the countries of Europe created alliances, America declared neutrality until 1917.

However, individual Americans did participate in the war before America's commitment.

John Jr. was married and twenty-two years old in August of 1914, when the opening salvos were fired. Having spent nineteen years of his life in England, he still felt a loyalty to the country of his birth. Within days he took a ship out of New York. He joined the 11th Hussars, an elite fighting unit of the English army, and soon found himself in the trenches of Belgium. There, he was shot in both legs and gassed. Unconscious, he was unaccounted for by his unit and declared dead. A representative of England's king mistakenly made a condolence call to his wife Clara. However, when she traveled overseas to claim his body, she found him alive. Amazingly, John recovered and was sent back into battle, this time to Mesopotamia (modern-day Iraq), fighting Germany's ally, the Ottoman Empire. He was again wounded and did not recover until 1919 (a year after the war ended).

The United States was still not at war when Harry turned eighteen in 1916. However, German U-boats controlled much of the Atlantic. Passenger ships were rare and unsafe for travel across the ocean. Harry's solution was to travel to Canada and join the Canadian army. This way, he had a better chance of actually making it to a *battlefield* before the war was over. He soon found himself in the Battle of Vimy Ridge in Northern France, where like his older brother, he suffered leg wounds and was gassed. In his case, the gas severely affected his lungs, and he remained in recovery in Canada until 1919.

In 1917, Fred turned 18, just as America was declaring war on Germany. He joined the American Expeditionary force and soon found himself "Over There," as popular American song proclaimed. One of the youngest in his unit, he blew a bugle, while also carrying a rifle as the American troops charged from trench to trench. In the end, the American presence changed the balance of power in the previously stagnant battlefront. The Allied side was victorious, and eventually, soldiers of every country returned to their homes. However, not all returned the same as they left.

In 1919, the three brothers united for the first time since 1914. The New Bedford newspapers gave front-page headlines to the return of the three brothers who had fought for three different countries against a common enemy. The article was full of tales of bravery and commendation from three different countries. It downplayed the sad downside of the story. John had lost a leg and would forever suffer discomfort. Gas had damaged Harry's lungs, and he would never breathe right again.

However, the article did end on a high note. John and Harry were Fred's biggest fans when he returned to playing soccer (as it was now called). They attended his matches and rooted for their youngest brother, who had returned unscathed. The article also mentioned, that happily, Fred was soon to be married. A

September 11, 1919 wedding date had been set for Fred Rostron (my grandfather) and Robena Pilling (my grandmother).

(1920 to 1930)

Brothers in Arms

"Through these fields of destruction,
Baptism of fire,
I've watched all your suffering,
As a battle raged high."

- Dire Straits

In 1998, journalist and author Tom Brokaw coined the phrase the "Greatest Generation" to describe those born in the first decades of the twentieth century. They had triumphed over so much adversity in their lives. They had been born into an era of great expectations and possibilities only to watch them vanish overnight.

Older members of this generation got to experience the excitement of the 1920s. It was a time of economic and technological growth. Construction boomed, and new roads now connected previously distant sections of the country. It was an era of dynamic artistic, social, and cultural change. People had access to cars, radios, and moving pictures with sound. They listened to jazz and danced to the Charleston. There was a feeling of being more modern than previous generations. The French called these years "The Crazy Times," but these good times in the United States will always be remembered as the "Roaring Twenties."

However, not everyone experienced this time equally. To the men and women of the "Greatest Generation" who were *actually born* in that decade, the great joy of the "Roaring Twenties" was stolen from them before they could even reach their teenage years. Instead, they were to suffer through some of the most challenging times this nation has ever known—without ever sharing in the frenzied happiness that their older peers had enjoyed.

By the late 1920s, Domenico and Filomena Cippitelli owned an entire block in South Jamaica, Queens. With hard work and sound financial decisions, the couple and their seven children prospered. They created a tiny enclave of family and friends who had all come from the same area of Italy. It had not been easy. At first, the Italian population that had settled there was met by the resentment of the existing Irish population that had only a few decades before suffered similar discrimination. Though both groups were Catholic, their churches were segregated, with the Italians not being allowed to worship at the same locations as the Irish.

Yet, the generation born in the twenties rejected this notion, and large groups of friends came to include anyone or any nationality. Their childhood in this little section of Queens seemed to portend a beautiful world ahead of them...until it all came crashing down around them on "Black Tuesday," October 29, 1929. Sanity would not return to this generation for almost two decades.

· · ·

Though Domenico and Filomena had not invested in the stock market, the Great Crash drove the country into depression, and that did affect them. Since most of their married children lost their jobs, they were forced to move back to their parents' home. At times, the number of people living in the three-bedroom house was well above a dozen. To support those not working, the employed pooled their money. It was not enough. Gradually, all of the Cippitelli family's houses, besides their personal home, were sold off. All of their accumulated wealth disappeared and the family struggled to survive.

Yet there was joy in the house. When their daughter Lucia moved back, she brought two young children, Domineco and Filomena's first grandchildren. Born in 1922 and 1923, Josephine and Philomena brought a youthful spirit to the chaos of a crowded house. What's more, they also brought their friends to play in the backyard. There were their cousins, the Longo children, and their friends, the Speduti and Vanacore kids. However, "Granny" (as everyone now called Filomena) also welcomed into the yard the children of McHale, Fox, and Tamny families. Forged in the depths of the depression and the fires of war, this generation of children did not see differences but rather new brothers and sisters. This group, born in the 1920s. would truly be the "Greatest Generation." This little corner of Queens seemed almost exclusively Italian and Irish, except one lone transplanted English boy from New Bedford.

(1930 to 1940)

The depression had also hit New England. With the universal lack of money in the United States, the demand for clothing produced in the New Bedford mills dried up. One by one, huge employers boarded up their factories. The immigrants who had arrived in the last twenty years found themselves on bread lines. However, Fred Rostron had another solution. Though brought up in a family of skilled textile workers, the sea was never far from those who lived in New Bedford, a whaling port. Fred would join the Merchant Marines and earn his living at sea. However, he soon realized that most opportunities to sail were to be found in the port of New York.

In 1930, Fred and Robena Rostron and their one surviving child, Billy, moved to Queens. Fred quickly secured a job on a commercial voyage to Amsterdam, leaving mother and child alone in a strange city. Fred spent the next twenty-five years at sea, voyaging to five continents and over thirty different countries. During World War II, he risked the German submarine attacks to deliver necessary goods to Europe. However, he never returned to his family. Perhaps it was the sorrow over the loss of his young daughter or the traumatic experience of France's trenches.

Conversely, it may have just been his wanderlust and desire to leave behind all commitments. Fred abandoned his wife and son to fend for themselves in a very unfamiliar area of New York. By the mid-1930s, Robena wished to return to her family in New Bedford. However, her son had bonded with the boys and girls of South Jamaica, and so, she stayed.

·   ·   ·

Somehow the Irish and Italian Catholic children had accepted as a brother this young white Anglo-Saxon Protestant boy with a funny accent. As the depression deepened and poverty stripped them of all but the barest necessities of life, they bonded in friendship. Very often, Filomena welcomed the neighborhood children into her backyard to play. It was a large yard by the neighborhood's standard, and the dozen or so boys and girls often frolicked in the open space, careful not tread on the grapevines used for the bootleg wine the family enjoyed. Usually, when all of the children returned to their homes, a lone straggler stayed for spaghetti and meatballs. Granny knew that Billy had no one to go home to as his mother worked double shifts to provide for her son.

Soon, the young boy found that Domenico and Filomena's eldest granddaughter was more than just a friend. From the moment that he had pulled her hair while sitting behind her in third grade, there had been an attraction between Billy and the girl everyone called Peppy. By 1939, they vowed that they would spend their lives together. To do this, Billy had to make a future for them. He joined the navy two years ahead of all his peers who would eventually sign up in the emotion created by the bombing of Pearl Harbor. With this head start, he was already a Chief Petty Officer in the medical corps when America entered the conflagration. This would prove fateful to his future.

(1940 – 1950)

Many have debated the morality of dropping atomic bombs on the Japanese cities of Hiroshima and Nagasaki. While hundreds of thousands died in those attacks, it did force the ultimate surrender of the Japanese. The alternative to this scenario was the estimation that one million American casualties would have been sustained if the United States had been forced into an invasion. There was no question on which side of the debate the troops who were heading toward Japan fell. When surrender was announced, there was great relief on the ships of the invasion armada.

With the end of the war, most American troops went home to their waiting families—but not all. An occupation force set up camp in the conquered country. However, they were not just there to enforce the peace but also to help heal the wounds of war. And so, it was that Chief Petty Officer William Rostron found himself tending to the many sick and dying citizens of Hiroshima. In a world where little was known or understood about the long-term effects of radiation, a group of Americans helped ease the pain of their former enemies. They were a band of brothers who had never lifted a rifle but fought a more dangerous war on foreign soil.

Chief Petty Officer Rostron returned home to his wife and had three children and ten grandchildren. However, he never got to see half of those grandchildren. Suffering from one mysterious illness after another, he was in and out of hospitals most of his adult life. Yet, he lasted longer than most of his brothers-in-arms. Through the years, he followed the never-ending roll call of obituaries of his fellow medics who had lived in the tents on the fields of Hiroshima. And soon, his turn came.

. . .

My father lived long enough for me to get to know him, but my children never did have that honor.

(1950 to 1960)

"My Father's Eyes"

"Bit by bit, I've realized,
That's when I need them,
That's when I need my father's eyes."

- Eric Clapton

My father never earned a degree. He did not even graduate high school. Instead, he chose to join the navy at age 17. Yet, despite his lack of formal education, he was a avid reader. When I was young and enamored with the newly popular phenomenon known as TV, he would always insist that it should not replace the habit of reading. Being a smug, know-it-all preteen, I argued this fact.

One day he sat me down with the TV in front of us and a book in his hand. We always watched "Gunsmoke" together, and he asked me what I saw on the screen at that very moment. I shrugged, and he pushed me harder to answer.

. . .

"What *exactly* did you see?"

"Well, the bad guy pulled out his gun and tried to shoot Marshal Dillon. But he was too slow, and the marshal shot him first."

Much to my distress, he turned off the TV. There were no such things as VCRs or DVRs, or streaming in those days, so this meant that we would miss the episode. However, I guess that there was a little bit of a teacher in my father. He then pulled out the western novel that he was reading at the time and started to read.

Jack Barton reached down toward his newly shined leather holster. His youthful hand tried to retrieve his 1947 Colt Walker Revolver. His palm had barely begun to caress the wooden stock of the gun when he realized that he was too late. His gun would never kill another human being. The nine notches carved into the wooden grip would forever be his final total.

The sheriff placed his gun back at his side, its task completed. He did not rejoice at the death of his foe. His lightning-fast reflexes had merely completed the job he was paid to do. There was no joy in killing for him. It was just something necessary.

I realized at the moment that I would be a lifelong reader. What I had seen on the screen was a momentarily flash of interest, nowhere near the emotional experience of the written word. Eventually, I was to begin a career that involved teaching reading and writing. I only hope that I instilled in my students some small semblance of the love of reading that I felt that day so long ago.

(1960 to 1970)

"I Saw It on TV"

"A young man from Boston said, 'Sail the new frontier,'
And we watched the dream dead-end in Dallas.
They buried innocence that year."

- John Fogerty

Officially, the 1950s ended at the stroke of midnight on December 31, 1959. If you were alive then, you know that fact is simply not true. The thoughts, values, and culture of the fifties lived on into the sixties. To be exact, they lived on until November 22, 1963. At that time, all of us were dragged, kicking and screaming, into a new era. JFK did indeed bring us to something he called the "New Frontier," but his death also brought us to the end of our innocence.

Gone were the times John Fogerty sang about in a song he called "I Saw It on TV." Gone were Howdy Doody, and Mighty Mouse, and all the other Saturday morning cartoons. Gone were teenagers hanging out at the malt shop. Gone was a lifestyle epitomized by shows like "Father Knows Best" and "Leave It to Beaver" with their clean-cut families who never dealt with real problems. Gone was the feel-good era. Gone also was hiding from the real world and its real problems.

When I was in grade school, we practiced huddling under our desks to shield us from a possible nuclear attack. In our youth, we bought into this false promise of safety. With age, I realized that I lived in New York City, and we were target number one for the "heathen commies" who were trying to take over the world. No ancient wooden desk was going to protect me from a direct hit by a Soviet nuclear missile. John F. Kennedy's assassination changed everything. Never again would I feel secure in this world. I knew what was going on because I saw it on TV.

There were peace protests, civil rights marches, and some really great music on the Ed Sullivan Show. We listened to the Beatles and the British Invasion bands and many one-hit-wonder garage bands that produced lovable but forgettable hit songs. We watched Motown groups croon beautiful melodies while simultaneously performing intricate dance moves.

And each night, we sat and watched the networks count those who had died that day Vietnam War. I know because I saw it all on TV.

I left my childhood behind at the same time that most of America did and grew up. The world had changed on that November day in Dallas. However, there was a positive side to all that. We all became more aware of right and wrong, and that indeed there was evil in this world and whatever form we thought it took, and it had to be confronted.

I was a teenager in the 1960s, and all these thoughts and feelings went through my mind. But, I was *a teenager* in the 1960s, and to paraphrase that wise seer John Fogerty again, "Annette had ears, I lusted in my heart." And indeed, I had had lusted for a girl who I only had seen wearing mouse ears on the "Mickey Mouse Club." To be more precise, I was attracted to anyone who was female. My damn hormones were raging!

It was the 1960s. The world, with me in it, was spinning and spiraling in a way it had never done before. I know...I saw it on TV.

The author recently completed a trilogy of novels steeped in the late 20th and early 21st centuries' music and culture. Band in the Wind, Sound of Redemption, and Brotherhood of Forever have received critical acclaim from Writers Digest, the Online Book Club Review, and many other reviewers. These books have found readership on four continents (North America, Europe, Australia, and Asia).

In the past, he has published over two dozen non-fiction articles in newspapers and magazines. These writings included four full-page op-eds in New York Newsday. He was also presented an award by Nelson DeMille for his historical fiction short story, "The Last Artifact." Recently, his short pieces have in published in nine Red Penguin anthologies:

Three of his short pieces were accepted into the Visible Ink anthologies in 2018, 2019, and 2020. Each year, a dozen works are chosen for reading and presentation on stage in New York City. In 2018, "Pretty Flamingo" was given this honor. As an encore, "In the Garden of Eden" was performed in 2019. In 2020, his short work "Ava's Bubble" was read by Tony and Emmy nominee Victor Garber on a nationally televised streaming show. All of these are available for viewing on www.williamjohnrostron.com.

In his previous career, the author instructed students from the ages of 9 to 90. In his life, he taught elementary school, middle school, high school, college, adult education, and teacher training. He holds degrees from Queens College, Stony Brook University, and Long Island University.

Born and raised in Queens, NY, William John Rostron now splits his time between his home on Long Island and traveling the country in his Tiffin motorhome. When not writing, he is busy completing a bucket list of travel adventures. In the past 16 years, he and his wife Marilyn have traveled 120,000 miles. These journeys have taken them to the 48 contiguous states, 133 national parks, all 30 major league baseball stadiums, 154 cities and towns, two Canadian provinces, and a variety of unusual experiences and locations. Many of these locations have served as backgrounds for his books.

He presently working on a novel, Lost in the Wind, and an anthology, A Flamingo Under the Carousel.

www.WilliamJohnRostron.com

ABOUT THE EDITOR

JK Larkin is a Long Island-based writer and recent graduate of Marymount Manhattan College. On top of his position as Literary Manager and Editor of *The Red Penguin Collection*, JK works at The Mary Louis Academy as the coach of their Speech & Debate Team, coaching students to perform excerpts of dramatic literature, prose, and poetry for weekly competitions on both the local and national levels. His body of work draws heavily upon themes of existentialism, morality, and the struggle to connect in a deeply divided world. Follow him at @jksnotkidding and @jklarkinart on Instagram, @jksnotkidding on TikTok, or @JKLarkinTM on Facebook to keep up to date with his artistic journey.

ALSO FROM THE RED PENGUIN COLLECTION

Realiteen: Reflections On Growing Up

What Lies Beyond: Sci-Fi Stories of the Future

A Trip For The Books

I Can't Find My Flashlight

The Moments

The Beauty Within—Stories of Spirituality, Faith and Love

'Tis The Season—Poems to Lift Your Holiday Spirits

We Made It!—Essays Reflecting On The New Year

Stand Out—The Best of The Red Penguin Collection, Vol. 1

It's The End Of The World As We Know It

A Heart Full of Love—A Collection of Romantic Short Stories

Made in the USA
Middletown, DE
16 September 2021

48322134R00093